Peirene

RAYMOND JEAN

TRANSLATED FROM THE FRENCH
BY ADRIANA HUNTER

La Lectrice

AUTHOR

Raymond Jean (1925–2012) wrote more than 40 books during his lifetime – novels, short-story collections and essays. He was awarded the Prix Goncourt de la nouvelle in 1983. His novella *La Lectrice* (*Reader for Hire*) became a cinema hit starring Miou-Miou. The film won the César Awards for Best Supporting Actor and was named the best feature at the 1988 Montreal World Film Festival.

TRANSLATOR

Adriana Hunter has translated over 50 books from French, including works by Agnès Desarthe, Véronique Ovaldé and Hervé Le Tellier. For Peirene, she has already translated *Beside the Sea* by Véronique Olmi (Peirene No 1), for which she won the 2011 Scott Moncrieff Prize, and *Under the Tripoli Sky* by Kamal Ben Hameda (Peirene No 15). Adriana's work has been shortlisted twice for the Independent Foreign Fiction Prize.

MEIKE ZIERVOGEL
PEIRENE PRESS

The premise of the story is brilliant: a woman who loves reading aloud acquires – without realizing – power over others. What's true for her clients becomes real for you, the reader of this book. As you turn the pages, think of Marie-Constance as the personification of reading itself. And I promise you an experience you will never forget.

First published in Great Britain in 2015 by
Peirene Press Ltd
17 Cheverton Road
London N19 3BB
www.peirenepress.com

First published under the original French-language title
La Lectrice © Actes Sud, 1986
This translation © Adriana Hunter, 2015

ISBN 978-1-908670-22-9

Designed by Sacha Davison Lunt
Photographic image by Adrian Brockwell / Alamy
Typeset by Tetragon, London
Printed and bound by T J International, Padstow, Cornwall

This project has been funded with support from the European
Commission. This publication reflects the views only of the author,
and the Commission cannot be held responsible for any use
which may be made of the information contained therein.

Co-funded by the
Creative Europe Programme
of the European Union

Peirene

RAYMOND JEAN

TRANSLATED FROM THE FRENCH
BY ADRIANA HUNTER

Reader
for Hire

'In every woman there is an element that has gone astray… and in every man an element of the ridiculous.'

JACQUES LACAN

Let me introduce myself: Marie-Constance G., thirty-four years old, one husband, no children, no profession. I listened to the sound of my own voice yesterday. It was in the little blue room in our apartment, the one we call the 'echo chamber'. I recited some verses of Baudelaire I happened to remember. It struck me that my voice was really rather nice. But can we truly hear ourselves?

Funnily enough, when I met up with my friend Françoise last week, she said to me: You have a wonderful voice, it's silly not to do something with it. A woman really needs an occupation these days... When we were at the Conservatoire you showed such talent... Why don't you put an ad in the papers offering to read to people in their own homes? Françoise is lovely but she often has these outlandish ideas. As far as she herself is concerned, she has her feet pretty firmly on the ground – she's a lawyer's secretary – but that makes her all the more inclined to project a whiff of romance and quirkiness on to other people. And this was certainly a quirky idea: being a private reader – at a time when talking books are readily available – like in the days of duchesses, tsarinas and genteel companions. Oh no, retorted Françoise, not at all. It would be very different nowadays, totally practical and concrete: for people who're ill, handicapped, old, single. A delightful prospect indeed. But I have to admit the thought of bachelors was entertaining. The idea grew on me.

*

Now I'm sitting facing the man at the agency who takes the copy for classified ads. He's chewing on an extinguished cigarette butt beneath his toothbrush moustache, his eyes pinned on me. It's difficult to put a spark into dead eyes, but he's having a go. It's not up to me to give you advice, he says, but if I were you... I wouldn't run an ad like that... I really wouldn't... specially not in a town like ours... So I ask him why. He nods his head, heaves a sigh, rereads my piece of paper, which he's fingering helplessly: 'Young woman available to read to you in your own home. Works of literature, non-fiction, any sort of book you like.' Then comes my telephone number. You'll have trouble... A typist sitting at a nearby table stops every now and then to squirt the contents of a pocket vaporizer into one of her nostrils. She takes these opportunities to watch us furtively, probably listening. He lowers his head and his voice: Believe me, I know my job... I reply tartly: I'm asking you to *run* the ad, not comment on it. He eyes me in silence, staring, then explains that a lot of newspapers, even the biggest ones, now publish somewhat dubious ads, and that mine could be... misconstrued. He goes back to his chewing and nodding. I tell him there's nothing dubious about my ad. More squirting from the typist. In that case, he says, you should take out the words 'Young woman'... And put what instead? He thinks about this, concentrates: And put 'Person'. Now I'm the one who's baffled: What do you mean, person? He still has my piece of paper in his hand, and he holds it further from his eyes, as if to get a clearer view of it, the cigarette stub quivering on his bottom lip. Yes, you should put: 'Person predisposed to read to you in your own home, offers their services, etc.' You see, 'person' is sexless! Slightly dazed, I reply that no one will understand what the ad is about with all that gobbledegook in it. He falls silent, piqued, then says brusquely: All right, if that's what you want, we'll run it as it is. After all, it's up to you. But at least don't give your telephone number, just have a box number at the newspaper if you want to limit the fallout... Believe me, these ads are my standard fare and there's nothing standard about what you're offering... He hands the piece of paper to the typist, not even glancing at her but looking vaguely disgusted, and asks her to type out the text three times for the three local newspapers. Then he picks up a calculator and works out my bill. I write a cheque, stand up and leave. Aware of his gaze lingering on my calves and my heels.

Now I've come to see the man I call my 'old master'. He isn't old. Barely in his sixties. Roll-neck sweater, tweed jacket, pipe, an expression like a good-natured dog with bright eyes. Dear Roland Sora is very relaxed and always seems delighted to see me. He was my tutor on my literature course fifteen years ago, and we've kept up an easy, trusting friendship. He'd set himself a rule never to sleep with his students, so I was never his mistress. But I could have been: all the signs were there. I come to have a chat with him in his office from time to time, and to ask his advice about things. If there are too many students queuing up to see him, he comes out with me and we drive somewhere like the local bistro for a cup of coffee. If he's free, I sit opposite him in his office.

That's what I'm doing today. The usual compliments. He says a kind word about the colour in my cheeks, how I look. I note – out loud – that his hair is going very silvery and it suits him. Then I outline my idea. I can tell he's taken aback but doesn't want to show it. Everything's possible, he says, so why not reading to people in their own homes? Seeing as you committed the unforgivable error of not finishing your course, which you were quite capable of completing, and you have no prospects or position, anything that gives you something to do is all to the good. But a classified ad? I mean, really! And what's wrong with a classified ad? I ask. He fills his pipe, tamps down the tobacco. Well, yes, why not? he mutters, but doesn't hide his scepticism. He doubts it will deliver a result, doubts I'll receive any replies. I tell him we'll soon see, but that I'd like some advice from him about the sorts of books I should choose for my listeners, should any materialize. He thinks about this, or pretends to, drawing on his pipe and blowing smoke rings. Whatever you do, don't suggest anything tedious: no great works, no Proust, no Robbe-Grillet. No poetry either, but easy things that go down well. Like the minor naturalists. They're precise, they have stories, events, facts... He's always had a thing about the 'minor naturalist writers'. I think he did his thesis on them back in the day. And I remember some tremendous lectures – rather theatrical, but well planned – he gave about them. I remind him about this and he smiles and looks a little dreamy for a moment, lost in the mists of his pipe smoke and memories. Then he gets up suddenly and goes over to the bookshelves to the right of his desk, saying, Why the *minor* naturalists? Why not the greats? Why not Maupassant? There's nothing better than Maupassant, believe me, Marie-Constance, for all ages, all tastes, all situations, all countries... He'd be perfect for what you have in mind... You definitely shouldn't be embarking on anything ambitious or pretentious... Sora takes a beautiful Maupassant edition from the shelves, an old book with a brown binding, and leafs through it, looking for something. You should choose supernatural short stories, he says, you're guaranteed success... And then he launches into a strange description of his early days as a teacher. He was in a high school out in the sticks where he'd been given younger classes that bored him to tears, meanwhile he was champing at the bit, longing to start a university career, and to kill the boredom he would devote long hours in the classroom to reading supernatural short stories to his pupils. It was a huge success. The kids were frightened but, because they loved being frightened, they revelled in it and ended up more attentive than they had ever managed to be for any other lesson. We've all heard teaching tales like that. I could take inspiration from it.

Apparently wanting to illustrate his point, he's leafing through the book, searching, then he finds what he must be looking for. There, he says, 'The Hand'. Do you know it? Everyone knows 'The Hand'. I admit that I don't remember it very clearly. 'The Hand', he says, is the story of an eccentric Englishman who moves to Corsica to get away from it all and hangs a rather mysterious hand on the wall of his house. The story is narrated by a judge to a group of women, who are of course quaking as they listen to him:

Several women had risen to their feet and drawn closer, and they stood there, their eyes hanging on the magistrate's clean-shaven face as he pronounced these solemn words. They shuddered and quivered, fraught with inquisitive fear, with the avid and insatiable need for horror that preys on their souls, torments them like a hunger...

He stops to say: *The avid and insatiable need for horror that preys on their souls* – wonderful stuff, isn't it? He's been reading in a deep, resonant voice. I watch his lips, the clean-shaven skin around his mouth. He skips a few lines and picks up the story a little further on. Ah, here's the Englishman, he says:

He was a big man with red hair and a red beard, very tall and very broad, a sort of polite, placid Hercules. He had none of the so-called British stiffness, and in French coloured with an English accent he thanked me energetically for my tact. In the space of a month, we had spoken together five or six times...

And now here's the hand!

... In the middle of the widest panel something strange attracted my attention. A black object stood out against a square of red velvet. I moved closer: it was a hand, a human hand. Not the clean white hand of a skeleton, but a blackened, desiccated hand, with yellow nails, muscles laid bare and traces of old blood. This blood looked

14

like dirt on the bones, which had been cleanly severed,
as if by an axe, towards the middle of the forearm...

He breaks off his reading, closes the book and waits for my reaction. As this isn't immediately forthcoming, he carries on speaking himself: Completely effective... the plot lines, granted, they're simplistic, pretty laboured... but it works... There, that's what you need to read, if you want to find listeners... a good reliable French author who knew how to engineer suspense and a thrill like no other. You'll have them hooked every time. He must be disappointed that I don't look entirely convinced. I am, in fact, but I'm wondering who I'll have an opportunity to read these horrors to. I'm having a lot of trouble picturing that.

He has put the book back on the shelf and is already thinking about something else. He suggests we have lunch together one of these days, and asks after Philippe. Philippe is my husband. Does he know about my plan? I say that he does know about it, but couldn't care less. Said without a trace of hostility towards Philippe. I really love him as much as one can love a husband, and I think he's absolutely spot on for his type: the busy but cool young researcher type, the aerological engineer, with no complications. But it's true: he couldn't care less. If I'm happy about something, he takes note. If I want my life to change, he takes note too. He's anything but obstructive. That's how I describe him to Roland: anything but obstructive. Roland replies that I don't know how lucky I am. Then he takes me by the arm and leads me out of his office to the little local bistro.

Those idiots have gone and put my ad in the 'Work at Home' section. At home, yes, but other people's, not mine. I thought this would snarl up the whole enterprise, would make it fail completely in fact. But to my surprise the first letter has just arrived from the agency. It's from a good woman with clumsy writing. She says her fourteen-year-old son is disabled, she takes care of him at home as best she can, but he needs contact with the outside world: she thought that maybe…

Major hesitation on my part, I have to say. I eventually make up my mind and go to see this woman. She's very welcoming, very much the tearfully attentive 'mummy'. In a matter of minutes I can tell she's actually truly unhappy and truly devoted to her child. None of which precludes a degree of practical common sense: she's quick to ask me my rates. That's an issue I haven't considered and I'm secretly annoyed with myself for this. When you advertise your services in a newspaper, you should have worked out your rates. Completely forgot. Thoughtless. Inexcusable. And, yes, what *are* my rates? That's something else I should have asked Roland Sora – he must have given private lessons as a young man. If I don't give the woman an answer, I won't look professional. I tell her my rates are under consideration and I will communicate them to her in writing shortly, in the form of a small brochure laying out my programmes, my methods and my scale of charges. She looks delighted. A bit of nerve has paid off.

She draws her chair closer to mine in the kitchen, where she has chosen to speak to me, and embarks on describing her son's 'difficult' circumstances. She has very curly hair, which smells of heated rollers, breath that has not been sweetened entirely successfully by toothpaste, and a spotless apron. Quite out of the blue, she tells me I'm charming and have made a very good impression on her, that I'm definitely the most suitable person (yes, *person*!) to give Eric some help. As if to emphasize her liking for me, she pulls her chair another few inches closer. This attitude feels all the more peculiar because, in the very first instance, her friendliness seemed not to exclude an element of suspicion. That's fallen away in a flash and now she's pouring her heart out. Her mouth is busy talking, her floppy lips moving very quickly, her breath coming in acidic wafts. A touching woman, in her rather milky forties.

She explains that Eric suffers from spasmodic paraplegia and is confined to a wheelchair. His condition is serious but curable, she adds. In any event, it has no effect on the boy's intelligence; he's very clever and outgoing. Three times a week he attends an institute where he receives specialist help as well as a general education. But, of course, when he's at home he's on his own and he gets bored. He has no friends. His father is very busy with his work for the SNCF railway company and hardly has any time to spend with him. As for her, she does what she can. But, well, you know what mothers are like… It's in their nature to be too obtrusive, too invasive… particularly for a child in these circumstances... I can tell I irritate him sometimes... He's so highly strung... which is why I thought someone different... a bit of reading, some entertainment... But perhaps you only work with adults?

I take a moment to think (secretly genuinely panicked by this unexpected situation, but determined not to show it), then I reply: No, with absolutely anyone. Her face lights up, she looks relieved. But almost immediately a little triangular crease forms between her eyebrows. There is a problem, she says. You see, my husband and I can't afford very much, he's only an administrator... Might social services pay your fees? I can tell she's going to mention rates again and am quick to cut her off: I'd be very surprised. I'm not a nurse or a psychotherapist or anything of that sort, but a *reader*, that's all, with no qualifications, no diploma, nothing. You did understand my ad, didn't you?

She leaps up from her chair, clasps her hands as if in prayer and raises her eyes to the ceiling ecstatically: A *reader*! How wonderful! And he does so love reading... literature... He's so perceptive, such an artist... Oh yes, you're exactly what we need!

I'm beginning to find her a bit exasperating. And I'm getting the distinct impression I've launched myself into a pool of quicksand. Obviously. Who's going to want a reader at home in this day and age if not the manic, the mad and the sick? To get it over with, I come right out and ask: Can I see him? I haven't gauged the impact these words will have. She starts shaking in every limb, repeating, See him? See him? I feel I've made a mistake and have revealed myself as something I swore, only moments ago, I was not: some sort of health professional. I spoke like a doctor. Clearly a strategic faux pas. I should have waited for her to take the initiative and introduce me to Eric. She would have taken her time, and precautions. Instead I've stupidly rushed things. I'm no good at this job, or any other. I'm no good at anything. I don't know anything about human relationships. Suddenly I want to get out, to run away and leave her there, her and her unfortunate boy. What's he going to be anyway? Down's syndrome? A miserable paraplegic? A great bobbing moon face? Some poor unreceptive creature I'll have to tell stories to? That man at the agency was right. Trouble. A load of shit. That's what I can expect. I'll never change.

She's got a grip on herself very quickly. And before I've even had time to see what she's doing, she's opened the door at the far end of the kitchen. She leads me into the next room. Another three steps and I'm standing in front of Eric. He can't have helped hearing our conversation through the wall. He must be either appalled or furious. Or otherwise he really is completely deaf. I close my eyes for a tenth of a second before looking at him. Then I open them. And see a nice smiling face. With a look of extraordinary assurance. At least, extraordinary in someone who's incapacitated. In fact, he looks totally adult. So much so that I wonder for a moment whether this isn't some sort of trick. Here he is in his chrome wheelchair, dressed in a kind of tracksuit which successfully hides his legs, all of his body actually, but his torso is very upright, robust even. Not in the least atrophied or hunched.

This is the lady, his mother says, introducing me. His rather ashen face goes quite pink and his smile broadens awkwardly, and I can now see the child emerging in these features which initially looked so like a man's.

In a way, I find that rather reassuring. I'm sure we're going to get along, Eric, I say. Is it OK if I call you Eric? He nods, as if petrified, incapable of producing the least sound. Of course you can, says his mother. I take my time, walk around the room, come back to the wheelchair. Do you like reading? I ask. Affirmative nods. Would you like to hear some stories? Same nods. For entertainment or for education? His mother is quick to intervene: Oh, education, of course, education... And then, all of sudden, Eric speaks up clearly and firmly: No, for entertainment, he says. Brief silence. Do you have any favourite authors? No, I don't, Eric says, you can choose them. We'll trust you, says his mother.

Before I leave I can't avoid being trapped in the kitchen again for quite a long time. Eric's mother tells me everything, how and when the problem started, her hopes of a cure, Eric's finer qualities and minor faults, as well as hers and her husband's, the cruelty of fate. I can feel her gratitude about to boil over in her voice and in her now-glistening eyes. You'd think she was expecting salvation from me. I have to drink a tepid cup of coffee. And nibble on a biscuit. I promise to come back the day after tomorrow, for the first session.

Two days later the temperature has changed. A spectacular Indian summer. People walking along the promenade seem to have reverted to a summery mood. The late season's sun filters through the already sparse foliage, casting a pretty, powdery light that makes blouses and dresses transparent. I myself have put on a light crêpe dress with a full skirt, and the first thing I do once I'm sitting facing Eric with my book is lift it up above my knees. His mother has put us in his bedroom, sitting opposite each other, him in his wheelchair and me in a low armchair with cushions. It's really very hot and, almost without realizing it, I fan the fabric to get some air to my legs. It seems this is the only thing in the room Eric can see, and this ordinary gesture has produced a peculiar concentration in him. I'm quick to show him the book I've brought, a new edition of Maupassant's short stories, published by Garnier-Flammarion, with an image on the cover of a Normandy peasant woman in her distinctive headdress, against a background of huddled village houses. And I tell him that I'm going to read him several of these stories, that they're all really exciting and full of surprises, just as incredible as anything he'll find in the illustrated books and comics I can see piled up on a stool between his wheelchair and the table with his medication. But these stories have the advantage of being written in good, simple, substantial French. He seems to be convinced, and increases his mute nods of approval, as he did during my first visit, but without taking his eyes off the hem of my dress, or my knees even, although they're not all that much on show. I then tell him we're going to start with a particularly unusual, almost supernatural story called 'The Hand'. I tell him that the title will soon be explained and that the story will keep him on the edge of his seat from start to finish.

He looks a little feverish but enthusiastic, impatient. I decide he's far better-natured than a good many boys his age. And he may be genuinely hungry to learn, to listen to something new deep in the loneliness of his handicap. What if this job I've just invented for myself could, after all, be of real help to one or two people... I start reading:

They stood in a circle around Monsieur Bermutier, the investigating magistrate, who was voicing his opinion about the mysterious Saint-Cloud affair. This inexplicable crime had had Paris in the grip of panic for the last month. No one could make head or tail of it...

I stop for a moment and look up from my book to tell Eric that if there are any words he has any sort of trouble with, he mustn't hesitate to interrupt me and ask me their meaning. *Investigating magistrate*, for example. Does he know exactly what an investigating magistrate is? An instant, perhaps slightly peeved reply: Yes, Miss, I do. He obviously does not want me treating him like a child. And, worse still, like a retarded child. I'm vaguely aware that I need to make certain adjustments to my assessment of him. Is that why I pull up my dress, uncovering a little more of my knees? Besides, the heat in this room really is something. Through the window I can see a branch, its leaves so still you'd think the air had never been so utterly without a breath of wind. Perhaps I should open the window. But it's no longer really the time of year for open windows. Eric's face is a little red and he's now keeping his eyes focused on my knees with the utmost determination. But he's no less attentive to my reading. He seems to be genuinely interested. He registers precisely everything that my voice (which I hope he finds pleasantly melodious, although I'm quite incapable of gauging its inflexions at the moment) offers to his ears. All the details of this unusual story, which is now describing the career of our Monsieur Bermutier, who was appointed as a magistrate one day in Corsica, in Ajaccio, *a small, white town, resting on the shores of a magnificent gulf, surrounded on every side by high mountains.* It is here that cases of vendettas frequently come to his attention and land on his desk:

> ... *some are sensational, some dramatic in the extreme, some ferocious or heroic. Among them we may observe the most perfect subjects for revenge imaginable, age-old hatreds briefly appeased but never extinguished, abominable trickery, assassinations that evolve into massacres and actions that are almost glorious. For two years now all the talk I have heard has been of the price of a life, and of the dreadful predisposition in Corsicans driving them to avenge any insult on the person who made it, on his or her descendants, kith and kin. I had seen old men, children and cousins with*

their throats slit, my head was filled with these tales of vendettas...

I stop, still concerned that Eric is following easily and has no problems understanding. Do you know the word *vendetta*? Quick-fire answer: Yes, Miss, I know it. I know what it is. I think I sense a hint of irritation this time. Odd boy. I feel he's now genuinely gripped by the story and is really listening, although he hasn't chosen to take his eyes off my legs. But at the same time there's nothing passive about him, something about him is urging me to get on with it, to carry on. Right. The magistrate meets the Englishman. We've reached the passage about the hand:

But in the middle of the widest panel something strange attracted my attention. A black object stood out against a square of red velvet...

I hear something like a deep sigh, followed swiftly by a chesty wheeze. It's as if the words *black object* and *square of red velvet* have provoked goodness knows what feeling of suffocation. What dread. Perhaps an amazed, admiring sort of dread. I look up at Eric. His eyes meet mine for a moment, as if begging me to keep reading, then they look away. So I carry on. The hand. The iron chain from which it hangs on the wall. The anxiety among neighbours and witnesses. Then one day, the dramatic event. The macabre discovery. The Englishman assassinated. As suspense goes, you have to say there's plenty. Roland Sora was right. You couldn't do better. Eric is fascinated. Or terrified. I feel caught up in it myself, led on by the lightly handled but razor-sharp violence of the sentences and their rhythm:

A shudder ran down my back, and my eyes darted up to the wall, to the place where I had previously seen the horrible skinned hand. It was no longer there. The chain dangled, broken. So I heaved myself towards the dead man, and found inside his tensed jaw one of the fingers of that missing hand, cut or rather sawn off by his teeth right on the second joint...

This time, it's a scream. Short but shrill. Eric has thrown his head back and is clutching the armrests of his wheelchair with both hands as if clinging to them. His eyes are bulging out of his head and a string of saliva is oozing from his lips. I put the book down hurriedly, go over to him and take his wrist. It makes no difference. His whole body is shaking. Shivers are running down his back and the worst of it is that his poor paralysed legs are thrusting forward, as if propelled by convulsions. I run a handkerchief over his mouth and forehead. But the door to his bedroom has been thrown open and his mother has come in. My God, she cries, what's going on? What is this?... She flashes me a look as sharp as a dagger and rushes over to her child, trying to hug him to her and knocking over a bottle of Mercurochrome, which breaks on the floor, forming a pool of red. She's shaking almost as violently as he is. I tell her she'd do better to find some sort of tranquillizer, a few drops of something we could give him to swallow, or an injection we could administer. She grows all the more frantic, saying she doesn't have anything like that, that he's never had a fit like this, saying she's going out of her mind, that we'll have to call for help, and treading in the pool of red.

In fact, Eric calms down, but it seems help is still needed. He's now prostrate, his face perfectly white, his mouth still foaming, his head lolling on his shoulder and his eyes rolled almost right back. He's stopped shaking but a spasm jolts the lower half of his body every ten seconds. I'm already at the telephone, calling for an ambulance. When she realizes this, Eric's mother is furious. Anything but the hospital, not the hospital… she says several times. She looks for an address book to find the number of a male nurse who knows Eric, gets the pages all muddled and starts tearing them, panicking. But whatever happened? she cries… What did you do? What did you do *to him*? I feel idiotic, caught out. I stammer, meanwhile running my hand over the child's forehead, slapping him gently to bring him round: I don't know, I was reading him a story… quite an affecting one, perhaps… then suddenly, this seizure, this fainting fit… Oh, my God, my God, she sobs, and now you're slapping him, you're finishing him off, you're killing him!

Luckily the ambulance is here. Two nurses and a stretcher-bearer arrive and immediately take charge of Eric, asking for an explanation of the state he's in. His mother supplies it. As soon as she's finished I think it helpful to repeat my inane words: I was reading to him… quite an affecting story, perhaps… One of the three men looks at me as if I were raving mad, a halfwit at best. They examine Eric for a moment, then give him an injection. Next, they lift him out of his wheelchair and carry him, without using the stretcher: like a parcel, a lump. He's slumped in the arms of the colossus carrying him. His mother wails, weeps, wrings her hands. A spectacular disaster.

I go to the hospital the very next morning, sure of an icy reception. But, as luck would have it, things seem to have more or less gone back to normal. In the duty doctor's office they tell me that at first they'd thought they should send Eric to intensive care, at least for the night. But it very soon became clear that, with the help of a few antispasmodics, he had recovered to a state of relative calm. In other words, his pulse and respiratory rate were normal, and he could spend the night in the room, despite his obviously feverish and delirious condition. He's much better now. His mother is by his bedside. I may go and see him.

When I go into the room – number 27, at the end of a long white corridor on the first floor of the children's neurological unit – I'm expecting the worst. But I'm greeted with a smile. The same smile as on the day we first met. He has more than a bit of colour in his cheeks, his face is incontrovertibly pink, almost too flushed. It's the fever, his mother says, getting to her feet and coming over to me. Nearly 104. Apparently it might stay like that for a few days, but there's nothing to worry about now. They've run all sorts of tests… She is completely transformed too, no longer appearing to feel any animosity towards me. No *memory* of it even, you could be forgiven for thinking. How strange. Unexpected.

Eric is still smiling. A raised area under the sheet towards the foot of the bed indicates that they must have put some sort of brace on his legs, but he doesn't seem to be bothered, doesn't give the impression of being in pain anyway. He looks at me intently. I can feel his gaze sidling towards my right hand, as if he thinks I'm holding something, or *should* be holding something, a book perhaps... the infamous, horrifying book. I'm suddenly struck by the ridiculous idea that he might want me to go on with the story... But my hand is empty. I haven't even brought a bag of sweets, nothing, not the tiniest little treat or the most modest of flowers, convinced that I would find Eric in a dreadful state and was running the risk of being thrown out of his room. Take a chair, says his mother, and sit yourself there.

I sit down near the bed and take Eric's hand. It's of course very warm. I say softly: Poor boy, I didn't think I'd put you in such a state... You must forgive me... He squeezes my hand, says nothing. I should be giving you quite a talking-to, his mother says, because we came close to disaster, but I should probably give myself a talking-to first. I didn't say enough about how sensitive he is, how vulnerable...

A nurse comes in, wielding a thermometer in one hand and, in the other, a small tray with a glass of water and two capsules on it. She's a tall, attractive, dark-haired woman, upright with high breasts and wide hips. She busies herself briefly with the temperature chart attached to the foot of the bed, then hands the thermometer to Eric. Turning to her, his mother says: This is the *person* in question! I feel I've been denounced, handed over to the vindictive hospital staff, and the nurse does actually change her expression, furrowing her brow severely. Ah, she says, it's you! What on earth did you read to him to produce such a shock? It's incredible, unbelievable!... I look away as she puts her hand under the covers to help Eric take his temperature. The child keeps his eyes unswervingly on me as if asking me not to say anything, to protect him, hoping for some complicity. He's still holding my hand, squeezes it. I say a few evasive words: Oh, you know... a run-of-the-mill story... I had no idea... She eyes me really suspiciously. All through the night, she says, he kept pointing at the wall opposite him, as if he could see something terrifying there... There, there, he kept saying... He held his arm out straight, pointing with his index finger... and disabled though he is, he even managed to sit up in bed so he could reach his arm out properly... as if he was having some horrible nightmare... Then, more tartly, as she drew out the thermometer: You ought to take precautions in your job...

I'm stunned, speechless. My job! What job? It's only ten days since I ran the ad. All at once I wonder what on earth I'm doing here, in this hospital. I suddenly want to get out and leave them all there. But my problems aren't over yet. The nurse is hardly out of the room before a doctor arrives, escorted by an assistant or an intern. Most likely some consultant doing his rounds. But no one introduces him to me, tells me what his name is. On the other hand, I'm introduced to him, and still in the same terms: the *person* in question, or something like that. I can tell straight away that he views me with a degree of aggressive curiosity (thinking to himself: Ah, it's you!). After half-heartedly examining Eric, checking that his condition is improving and giving a few brief instructions, he asks me to come and see him for a minute in his office.

The office is an utterly sinister white room with a bare light bulb hanging from the ceiling, an old hatstand and a desk laden with papers, pamphlets and tired-looking books. He asks me to sit facing him and stares at me for some time. Then comes straight to the point. You're out of your mind, my dear! he says. Do you know what that child came close to? Encephalitis. You didn't take into account how ill he is, how badly incapacitated, a particularly fragile case... Are you a responsible adult? Are you? I mumble a few vague words, trying to make it clear that, if there was any fault on my part, it was due to inexperience, and that, alas, I have neither qualifications nor experience... He coolly leaves me to dig myself deeper and deeper into a hole. He's a stout, broad-shouldered man with a slightly chubby face, crew-cut hair and penetrating eyes. I feel as if he's literally undressing me with those eyes. But, imagine my surprise, suddenly he's the one getting undressed. He unbuttons and removes his white coat in a sequence of hurried gestures and, to my astonishment, is now standing in front of me in blue underpants and blue socks. He starts walking around me in his smalls and says: Do you mind if I change? I don't answer. He carries on circling, taking his time, lighting a cigarette to prove he's in no hurry. Then he hangs his white coat on the hatstand, heads towards a cupboard at the back of the room, opens it and takes out a shirt and jacket on a hanger, a pair of trousers and a tie. He talks to me as he puts on these various items of clothing: He had visions, hallucinations all night... He kept pointing at the wall... talking about a hand... What *was* this story you read to him? Just a short story of Maupassant's,

I reply. He's put on his trousers now and is tying his tie in front of a small mirror on the inside of the cupboard door. Maupassant, he says, Maupassant… Do you know how Maupassant ended up?… AIDS!… Anyway, in his day they called it cerebral fever, the sort of thing you nearly inflicted on that poor boy. Don't you think he's suffering enough as it is? You don't understand, his entire nervous system is wired… In future—

Still in my chair and without looking at him, I interrupt him: There won't be a future. Professor Dague – because that's his name – is now fully dressed, with his tie done up, a proper gentleman. He crushes his cigarette in the ashtray, lights another. You smoke too much, I say, getting to my feet. Caught off guard, he grants me a hint of a smile. He takes my arm: That boy's waiting to see you. He actually really likes you, is very fond of you… You should be able to help him… His tone has suddenly become friendly, attentive. I can feel his warm tobacco-laden breath on my neck. Fond of me, I say, he doesn't know me! I'm wondering which of us all is the maddest.

But, oddly, I let him persuade me. I go back to room 27 and sit down beside the bed. Eric takes my hand with an eagerness that leaves no room for doubt. His feverish eyes stay trained on mine. He's adamant that you should come back, his mother confirms. It was all just a misunderstanding, a mistake… We're really relying on you… He does so love reading!

I'm in the echo chamber. In my hand is a letter. The second letter, it's just arrived from the go-between newspaper. I hardly dare open it, it looks so peculiar. Blue, like the walls of my room. Vaguely perfumed, it seems, but that may be an illusion on my part. The stamp stuck on upside down. The writing elongated, exhausted. On the back are the words: La Générale Dumesnil (or Dumézil, the letters are particularly shaky and overlapping), rue des Rives-Vertes. I'm perplexed, anxious. The smart part of town. A 'générale'. I really will have to play the part of a reader from a bygone age. It was bound to happen. But so soon! Oh well, that's my bad luck.

Yes, the envelope is definitely perfumed. A slightly stale patchouli. I open it all the same and read it. Sure enough, this woman is a general's widow. She's eighty years old. She spends most of her time in bed. She's bored. She'd like someone to come and read to her. The letter isn't very easy to decipher. The writing buckles dramatically, especially at the ends of lines, as is often the case with older people whose eyes and fingers aren't what they used to be. But this missive still has something authoritative about it and a surprising dignity. There must be a whiff of aristocracy about the old lady. Besides, at the end she asks me about the terms of *my employ*, proof that she sees a reader as a servant. I say the words out loud a couple of times in the room – *my employ, my employ* – like the character

Sganarelle, a role I've played. The walls throw back an echo of the words, multiplied again and again, almost ad infinitum, with a long reverberation on that open *oy*. How funny. Comical even. I used to love playing Molière, and was apparently good at it, particularly the servant girls (not just Sganarelle). Here's an opportunity to be a servant. But what should I read to Madame la Générale? At eighty, she probably ought to steer clear of Maupassant's supernatural stories. Otherwise it won't be hospital but the morgue. I'd better not make a speciality of killing off my customers.

I didn't actually read all of the letter, perhaps for want of enthusiasm or conviction, a subconscious semi-denial. There's a postscript that's even more trying to decipher than the rest and I didn't look at it at first. In it La Générale says this: I forgot to point out that I am not on good terms with most of my family because of my political views, which illuminates my loneliness. For obvious reasons I find this intriguing. Is La Générale a barmy old reactionary? The *which illuminates my loneliness* is extraordinarily odd. It seems to say the exact opposite of what it wants to mean. Probably: *which explains my loneliness*. Could this awkwardness, this inaccuracy, be down to a limping familiarity with the French language? It could. Then I notice something I hadn't spotted before: the letter is signed Générale Dumesnil, née Countess Pázmány, a foreign name, Hungarian perhaps... I can hear the words ringing in my ear: *which illuminates my loneliness*. I repeat them several times. The blue walls throw them back at me. I close my eyes and picture a lamp glowing in a dark cellar. Its vaulted ceiling illuminated by the flickering light. Loneliness illuminated by a candle, by candlelight, like in Georges de La Tour's paintings. Night-time, all that darkness and the back-lighting effect going on behind my eyelids.

Here I am, holding the letter, feeling truly overwhelmed. Do I have to go to this countess? What sort of impossible situation am I going to end up in this time? The smell of patchouli wafts up to my nostrils; it's a bit sickly. Who does this coquettish old girl think she is? I'm so comfortable right here. Some days I think I'd do better never to leave the house.

I decide I should pay another visit to my 'old master'. He doesn't seem in a terribly good mood today. Or even in the best of health. Bags have developed under his eyes. And his brow is knitted. It's exam time, marking time, a time when dissertations come in from every direction. I ask, just to make conversation, whether he's still playing tennis. No, he retorts rather curtly, I go jogging now. For a moment I picture him in his tracksuit running along an avenue of silver birches, or plane trees, on a carpet of the first fallen leaves, sweating, puffing (no: trying to regulate his breathing), his elbows tucked in to his body. But his brow has already eased. No doubt about it, I've proved it yet again: he's glad to see me, even when I'm disturbing him. He doesn't let it show straight away, but it's always clear eventually. I'm very glad too. I find him reassuring. And, in my current confusion, I need his advice.

I start by telling him about Eric. He listens while signing some papers, then suddenly puts down his pen and stares at me for some time, looking genuinely perplexed. It feels as if he finds the story completely ridiculous. But I haven't altered it a jot, or exaggerated at all. It's your fault, I tell him, because it was you who made me choose Maupassant's short story 'The Hand' for my first reading. That's true, he says, getting to his feet abruptly, I did! He stuffs his pipe. I did, it's my fault! But perhaps you should have taken into account who your listener was. How sensitive he was, his condition… don't you think? Wouldn't that have been sensible? He's pacing swiftly about his office, pipe in hand, then in his mouth. He sits back down, looks at me again. You know perfectly well there's a text–reader connection that can't be overlooked. I get the feeling that this is *the professor* speaking and I feel like laughing. I smother the urge by looking away as if I feel guilty.

When I tell him Eric is now much better and even wants me to carry on being his reader, with his mother's consent, he's the one who looks highly amused. I'm not surprised, he says. You always end up wrapping people around your little finger! But maybe it was your voice that completely won him over. A young man… and one who's trapped inside his own body… You have such beautiful intonations… Oh! I say. He stands up, comes over to me and puts a hand on my shoulder. I sense this is the right moment to reveal the second approach I've had. Right, he says, interesting, but this time you'll have to take precautions, not make any wrong moves, because she may be a batty old woman but she may also be a rich widow, and then you're bound to be on the way to a lucrative career. He's obviously making fun of me, but not unkindly. I'm floundering, not sure what to say, when he whisks away from my shoulder and springs towards his bookcase, as he did the other day. Another old book with a brown cover. A novel by Zola this time. He'll never get beyond his naturalists! He searches, flicks, leafs, with the elegant gestures of those who have read a great deal and know they will soon flush out the required page. Zola's *The Masterpiece*! he cries. A wonderful book, you must know it. A magnificent but tragic portrait of a painter, it could be Cézanne... Anyway, right from the start there's a story about a funny scrap of a girl called Christine. The hero finds her outside his studio one evening in the pouring rain. He takes her in, gets her to talk. She tells him she's just arrived in Paris from the country – completely alone, completely lost, completely terrified – in order to be... to be what?... Ah, to be what?... To be a reader for a general's widow! Right, here's the passage. He tilts the book towards the light, towards the window that looks out over the campus lawns.

> *In only a few words, Christine told her story. She had left Clermont the previous morning to come to Paris, where she was to take the position of reader for a general's widow, Madame Vanzade, a very wealthy old woman who lived in Passy. The train was scheduled to arrive at ten past nine and all the arrangements had been made. A chambermaid was to meet her, they had even exchanged letters agreeing on how she could be identified, by a grey feather in her black hat...*

Roland Sora looks very satisfied to have found these few lines of text. It's a perfect match, he says, you're taking the position of reader for a general's widow. The best thing would be to read her this passage, this book. It would be perfect! I feel very wary. What if Zola has worse surprises than Maupassant's in store for me? These writers who deal in *realism* are the ones who come up with the most outlandish things. And perhaps my old Générale doesn't want to be shown a ridiculous reflection of herself, but would prefer refined or poetic material to ease the pains of her advanced years. And actually, here I am forgetting she's also a Hungarian countess: perhaps she'd like Hungarian authors... Roland has come back over to me, holding the closed book in his left hand. With his right hand he straightens a few stray hairs in the middle of my fringe. You should wear a hat with a grey feather! he says.

I ask him whether he knows any Hungarian authors. I haven't explained the reason for my question, though, so he studies me with the rather suspicious sort of astonishment he reserves for when I disconcert him (and, sadly, that happens quite often). Petőfi, he says... Then, as if finding that too banal for a university professor, he thinks for a moment and goes on to add, György Konrád, an excellent novelist... Or Somlyó, a wonderful poet... I ask him to write them down for me, but all of a sudden he claps his hand to his forehead. The Hungarian authors have just reminded him he has an important thesis about comparative literature to read for tomorrow and he practically shovels me out. With his most charming smile, mind you. He even takes his thoughtfulness so far as to escort me to the end of the corridor. A few students smile at him. A colleague gives him a friendly wave. I feel a slight nostalgia for this place where I was once rather at home. But it's changed. There used to be posters and tracts in every direction, and a smell of revolution. Now there are just Styrofoam cups and scraps of old tissues on the floor, and a smell of Coca-Cola.

Another reading session with Eric. Everything goes well this time. He wanted more Maupassant, as if to prove he wasn't afraid of the author and was not ready to give up on him. But this time I've chosen a perfectly innocuous story, 'The Necklace', which I remember well, having read it at some time as a teenager. I can't recall exactly where or when, but I can picture a barn on a rainy day, me sitting in the straw reading that story. It's all about a party and some spectacular diamonds. I felt they were glittering right there in among the straw that was prickling my thighs. The woman wearing them – or, to be more accurate, who had borrowed them to wear them – was radiant. Giddy with happiness and pleasure. And now, all of a sudden, right in front of this incapacitated boy:

She danced deliriously, with exhilaration, intoxicated by the pleasure, her mind a blur, triumphing in her beauty, glorying in her success, in a sort of cloud of happiness conjured by all the compliments, all the admiration, all the desires awakened, and by a victory so complete and so very dear to every woman's heart…

I can tell Eric is positively quivering. I even wonder whether I've made a bad choice again, the inverse of my previous mistake: the image of this woman, her giddiness… But no, he's very calm. He is quivering in anticipation of a happiness he hasn't experienced. The words *exhilaration, intoxicated, desires awakened* are strong ones for this child, who is obviously intelligent and who – I now know, I know only too well – is hypersensitive. My sensibilities were sharply awakened too, back in that barn while the rain fell hot and heavy. (Where was it? When was it?) Why shouldn't he have a right to life? To the intoxication of life?

I'm wearing jeans today and I suddenly get the feeling he's very disappointed. It may be a false impression, or an absurd one, or an utterly subjective one. But from the way he's moving his head and letting his eyes wander, hovering over me, then snatching them away as if looking at something inside his head, with a peculiar combination of embarrassment and impatience, I get the feeling he's not pleased that my legs are bundled up in this sturdy fabric.

After a while the story seems to be having an effect. Yes, he's listening! I'm not reading for nothing. I'm doing it for a reason. In fact, it's almost as if Eric registers every little word I utter, like the sensitive point of a seismograph. Yes, a secret trembling, captured with extraordinary precision: that's the sort of attention he's paying to this text by the minor master Maupassant, a text which, in my opinion, is on the bland side but which describes shimmering, glistening things. What matters is not how the words are written, but how they come out of my mouth and my body. In the same way that it mattered how they danced before my eyes back there in that barn, in the straw, while the rain fell. I feel a great surge of pity for this paraplegic child, a surge of tenderness that he doesn't even suspect. Why shouldn't he have a right to happiness, to the rain and the sun?

At Générale Dumesnil's house I am greeted by a maid-servant. I won't use a more ordinary word because, in her starched apron, she really does have some style and a fairly high opinion of herself. She shows me into a bedroom, where the only thing I can see is a bed. A vast, disproportionate bed that seems to take up the entire room. And here, in an accumulation of cushions and books, is La Générale. There is also a large, almost mauve-coloured pedigree cat in among the blankets. La Générale waves me over and says, Come in, come in, Nouchka. Come closer. Sit yourself down. Why Nouchka? Perhaps a habit and a sign of courtesy, but I make a point of not considering the question. The only thing I notice for now is her accent, which is clearly from Central Europe, probably Hungary, and which is especially noticeable in the rolling way she pronounced the name Nouchka. She looks very pleased to see me; she invites me to sit on a rather low stool, dismisses the servant and sets about explaining her situation and her problems.

Her eighty years have clearly not compromised her robust character and she is obviously one of those self-indulgent people whose gushing onslaught of confidences you have to accept with resignation. I brace myself, duly resigned, while maintaining outward signs of perfect politeness, because I feel my new profession is in the process of 'settling in'. With a sweeping gesture of the back of her hand, La Générale draws my attention to all the books scattered over her bed and says that, alas, she can no longer read them, her eyes are forsaking her. She reaches across to take three different pairs of glasses from the bedside table and throws them down on to the covers with something close to disgust: not one of the three pairs is of any help to her now. She's going blind. Which I promptly realize is obvious from the sort of fog in her eyes, although they are still very beautiful and very pale, but also from the way she looks just to one side of me when she appears to be peering right at me. Oh yes, she says, *cataracts*! She pronounces this word in such a gorgeous, rolling, utterly Magyar way that this time there is no doubt about her origins. Reading was her passion. But not just any reading. It's important that I understand this, because she's expecting me to compensate for her eyes' failings. No, not just any old books, but her favourite authors, and one in particular: Marx.

I ask her to repeat herself, afraid I've misheard because of her accent. But that's what it was: Marx. Yes, Marx, she says, and secondarily (here again, a magnificent rolling of that adverb) Lenin. Realizing that I am hesitating, she steeples her knees under the covers to move the blankets and cushions, shoo away the cat and make some of the books topple towards me. I watch them tumble pell-mell at my feet: *Capital*, *The German Ideology*, *Materialism and Empirio-Criticism*. Now gauging the extent of my surprise, she launches into an account of her life and her views, not giving me the chance to utter a single word.

She is a countess, a genuine Hungarian countess: Countess Pázmány (she signed her letter to me as such, she does hope I noticed). Her husband was a French officer, Général

43

Dumesnil, posted to Budapest, where they met before the war. He was a military attaché (and a mere lieutenant at the time) and she was viewed as one of the most feted women among the Hungarian aristocracy. She was introduced to her future husband at a ball when she was wearing one of her most precious heirlooms (a delicious rolling sound, deep and yet also fluty), a sparkling necklace. It was love at first sight. They were married and were happy together. Until the day she realized that all these military attachés were just spies and double agents, camouflaged secret-service agents working... for whose benefit? For the CIA (they may not have said CIA at the time, but it amounted to the same thing). She was convinced of it, perfectly convinced, and she could prove it. She'd watched her husband at work at fairly close quarters. The 1949 revolution had swept all that aside. She was still there when the socialist bloc was set up, and she saw the victory of the Workers' Party. In the heat of the moment, like everyone else, she was frightened, and her husband asked to be sent back to France – he was by then a general and had been posted back to Budapest after the war, but he didn't feel at all comfortable being married to a countess and thought things were about to take a very nasty turn for her and for him. They had come to France and taken early retirement in this dismal little town. France had always felt cramped to her. But here, in this hole, it couldn't have been any worse. In hindsight and seen from this distance, it felt as if, in comparison, her own country had been brought to life by a historical upheaval as powerful as a natural catastrophe (she gives these words another magnificent Magyar roll, then pauses as if exhausted by the effort, catches her breath...). She could now gauge the scope of its effect; there were casualties, of course, but you can't make an omelette without breaking eggs. In any event, she would never budge now. She could be insulted, dragged through the mud, labelled a *Red* (which was what her husband said), but she was convinced of the benefits of this historical upheaval... For good measure, she adds that, yes, the repression of the 1956 Uprising was difficult and painful, but sadly there had been no choice: it was that or counter-revolution... There was no question of allowing a counter-revolution... Kádár had done the right thing, he was a great man... and this was proved by the fact that he had stayed in power ever since and was now respected all over the world... a hero... perhaps even a saint...

To my amazement, she leans towards the drawer in her bedside table, takes out a photograph of Kádár and kisses his forehead as she might an icon or a religious image. He saved them from the unthinkable, she says, the unthinkable! And he displayed an unusually calm, firm approach. You can see it in the forceful set of his chin, from his jaw and the rather high cheekbones you sometimes get in my country... They say we're a race of Eskimos, you know, of Lapps, something like that, right in the heart of Europe...

She stops to ring a bell. She turns to the maidservant, who has just appeared rather sulkily, and asks her to bring us some tea, and this won't be from Lapland or Hungary, she laughs, but very good orange-flavoured tea from Sri Lanka. She usually has at least six cups of it a day. She does hope I'd like to have some with her, now that I'm her appointed, paid reader (she's the one to say appointed, without the least rolling sound, obviously, but with the elongated inflections she masters so adeptly). Because we shall understand each other well. She likes me. I really am exactly what she needs (although I haven't actually opened my mouth, or hardly at all). It goes without saying, we'll have to see whether I can read Marx properly. Because, Nouchka, she says, without Marx, the whole little history lesson I've just given you would have absolutely no reason to exist, considering that the impressive events that so completely reshaped my country wouldn't even have been conceived. So, we're going to have a trial run! She reaches across the blankets for a book that she seems to recognize by touch alone, and hands it to me, saying authoritatively and without the least hesitation, Page 125, read! It's the *Anti-Dühring*, a passage I never tire of hearing… I take the book, open it at the appropriate page and ask whether it's the passage indicated with a cross. Yes, she says, a cross, and there should be a note in the margin: *Morals have always been class morals*. That is the subject of this passage… magnificently handled… Go on, start reading! So I start:

> *When we see that the three classes in modern society (the feudal aristocracy, the middle class and the proletariat) each have their own morals, we can only draw one conclusion from this fact, and that is that, consciously or unconsciously, people ultimately draw their ideas of morality from the material conditions that underpin their social class, from the economic conditions of their output and their exchanges…*

What a marvel! she exclaims. I'd rather you read it in German or in the Russian translation by Lunacharsky, because this version's a bit halting, but obviously you can't. It doesn't matter. The important thing is the ideas and, as you can see, they're so right... Ah, the three classes... the feudal aristocracy... I'm familiar with that, you know, I'm from there... I know the boyars... I know what I'm talking about, and I know what *he's* talking about... I've more than dipped my big toe in all that, bathed in it, wallowed in it. You have no idea what it's like when the rot sets in... when the rot sets in to social class... Morality... their morality was a beautiful thing...

I'm all the more astonished, because I found the text lethally boring and couldn't envisage reading on without a deep-seated feeling of apprehension. But she seems delighted. Overjoyed. She's nestled between her cushions, whispering, I never tire of listening to it! Then she scoots abruptly down into her bed, gives me a wave of her hand and says: Perfect! The trial was conclusive. You have a beautiful, clear voice with good resonance, nicely in keeping. You will come and read Marx to me twice a week, for two hours each time, and you will be paid 200 francs a session. But for now you'll have to excuse me, I need to sleep. And she promptly turns on to her side, pulls the blankets over her head and falls asleep.

The maidservant comes in with the orange-flavoured tea. It looks as if I shall be drinking it on my own. Unless this woman, this pinched and starched tray-bearer, is going to partake of it with me. Which is what happens. We understand one thing at least: the fact that we are both servants, on the same footing. Have some, she tells me. I think you're right for her, so now we can set the dates and times.

I have some. Tepid coffee last week. Tea today. My profession's becoming rather social. But my rates are beginning to look more established. I've got what I wanted.

Perhaps the time has come for me to describe myself. I'm on the tall side, slim in my upper body, wider lower down. I have black hair with flashes of auburn, cut into a curved fringe over my forehead and drawn into a French pleat at the back. Green eyes. A pointy, slightly sharp face which was described as unattractive when I was a little girl. I remember crying for ages one day when a cousin referred to me as an 'abominable parrot'. I was left with an acute awareness that some people might think I look like a bird. Even if I do have a slightly hooked nose, I actually have full, very cushiony lips, and I think my complexion is more like peaches than feathers.

To get back to my body, my neck rises tall above my shoulders, my arms are slim, my waist is slim and my breasts are nicely separated – a little too copious for my chest, granted, but I've found this to be a considerable asset in plenty of situations, having managed to view it as a disadvantage for a long time. In any event, standing naked in front of the mirror, I think I make a pretty favourable impression, at least down to my belt line. Below that, as I've already said, things are very different. I have pronounced hips and this gives me a wide stomach and full buttocks. That too can be an asset. But there was a time in my life when I wasn't terribly willing to wear trousers and jeans, which went against the fashion. I wear them nowadays, even tight ones. Apparently they really suit me, according to those who know. I've forgotten a detail about my stomach, and it's a real distinguishing feature (but my identity card doesn't mention it): instead of being perfectly in the middle, like everyone else's, my navel is slightly off-centre, up and to the left. Which leaves us with my legs. My thighs are a bit too full as well, but when it comes to my knees, calves and ankles, everything is perfect, again according to those who know.

My body, I'd like to point out, is regularly maintained by sessions of gentle gymnastics taught to me by Françoise, and overall I feel in excellent shape, despite a few vague rumplings and crumplings that I thought I felt here and there the minute I hit thirty. Anyone looking at me gets an impression of good health and, because I'm cheerful, there's something reassuring about my appearance – invigorating even, if we are to believe my husband, Philippe. Unfortunately, some people detect an inexplicable insolence in my chirpiness. I'm not insolent at all. I am as I am. A woman probably like any other, but a woman, yes.

Do I have the necessary qualities to be a good reader? That's clearly quite another problem. Perhaps, in order to look serious enough, I should wear glasses. Actually, I do wear glasses a lot, sunglasses. But I expect I'd need real ones, even if they had clear glass lenses. I'll have to think about that.

In fact, I decide to discuss the glasses idea with Roland Sora. On this particular day he has some time to himself and we have our chat in a cafeteria next to the faculty building. It's still very warm, but autumn is definitely here: through the glass wall along the right-hand side of the cafeteria, I can see dead leaves accumulating on the lawn, and the grass is yellowing. Mind you, there are a few students sitting reading here and there, out in the fresh air, as if it were still summer.

We've taken a coffee and a slice of tart each. Roland very sweetly says that glasses are bound to suit me well and would give me a little intellectual touch I may lack, therefore increasing my credibility (that's his word, not mine) in my new occupation. Unfortunately, he can't think of an optician I could ask for fake glasses without causing a degree of consternation. I tell him I couldn't care less if I cause consternation. Or perhaps, he says dreamily, bringing his coffee cup up to his lips and gazing into the middle distance, or perhaps: bluish, tinted, you need to ask for non-corrective lenses but with a slight blue tint... I tell him the easiest thing would be just to go to a props supplier. He puts down his cup and seems to hesitate, as if not entirely sure of the spirit in which I said this. I can tell he's slightly on the defensive; perhaps he thinks I'm making fun of him. Then he replies: Why not? You're used to the stage, after all, Marie-Constance.

He looks at his watch. I suddenly get the feeling that this conversation about glasses is going to come to an abrupt end or go around in circles. Better switch to something more concrete. Shall I show him the letter I received yesterday? The third letter I've had since my ad appeared. I haven't mentioned it to anyone yet, not to Philippe or to Françoise. It's a different sort of letter this time, typed. And from a man. It feels important. It's right here in my handbag. In a way, it makes my heart beat harder, because there's an element of the unknown to it, but also because there's something about it that is utterly serious and utterly official. And I rather like being taken seriously. I read it out loud, to impress Roland:

Dear Madame,

I noticed your advertisement in the local paper a few days ago. As Managing Director of a large company, I have a very busy life. In the very few free moments afforded by my schedule, I thought that the 'reading' sessions you are offering might help perfect my knowledge of cultural affairs, something which has become increasingly indispensible these days, particularly in my fields of activity and responsibility, and something I do not have the leisure to acquire by any other means. In other words, I should like to 'keep abreast' of things, to know what is being read, what is being said, what people are discussing. I will abide by your conditions.

If this offer is acceptable to you, Mademoiselle, I would be grateful if you would kindly contact me, etc.

I glance up to gauge the letter's effect. Roland doesn't look terribly pleased. More on the sullen side even. He finishes his last scrap of tart with a waggle of his head and an extremely suspicious expression on his face. I was almost sure he would feel like this, but I've played the card anyway. If I were you, he says, I'd be cautious. Oh, why? Because he says *Mademoiselle* at the end having said *Madame* at the beginning, unless that was your mistake... No, it's not my mistake. He definitely did write *Madame* at the beginning of the letter and *Mademoiselle* as he signed off, that's a fact. A significant fact, says Roland, not an innocent slip-up at all. Right, so? So nothing, caution, that's all. But Roland's very swiftly changed his tone now, the first shock must have passed: A managing director, he says, no less! I pick up on this, saying it's an unhoped-for opportunity, a completely unexpected turn of events. That ad in the paper was definitely a very good idea, despite what various people might have thought, and here was the evidence to prove it. I'm really on the way to having a proper clientele.

But wait, be cautious! Roland Sora reiterates. It may be a trap. This man may have ideas in the back of his mind. You're not completely stupid, are you? You do see what I mean? I pretend to think about this. Yes, I see, I do see... I turn the letter over and over in my hand. He must think I'm joking, putting on a performance for him, but I really am pleased, completely gratified by this proposal. It's not something I've invented. It's right here, in my hand, nice and clear, nice and distinct, nicely typed out, probably by some impeccably trained secretary.

Roland is actually now glancing slightly askance at the envelope and trying to read the letterhead. I come to his rescue. The company's called Nickeloid, I tell him. I have to admit that when I saw that it didn't occur to me to think... I thought it was for Philippe, or a bill, or I don't know quite what... Nickeloid? What can that be? What do you think? I ask. He's taken the envelope from me and is looking at it suspiciously. I don't know, but I hope it's a real company... and a real managing director... a managing director who wants to reinvent himself, buying himself an instant cultural education to do better in his business transactions... Business, there you are, that's the word... It's all about business... and it only remains for me to hope that this particular business transaction is fruitful for you, dear Marie-Constance. I hope that with all my heart, but I'll say it again: Caution! Keep your eyes open! With men, you never know... I act as if I don't fully understand: With men?... Yes, he says, irritated, with men, the male of the species!

I thank him for his fatherly advice. But he slips in one last suspicion. How come, he says, this letter's arrived so late, so long after the advertisement was printed, because, correct me if I'm wrong, it's now a good three weeks since it was published, isn't it? He counts on his fingers: the week with the little handicapped boy, the week with La Générale, the hospital week, or perhaps it was the other way around, I've forgotten the exact order of events... You're already an old hand in this profession, nearly a month... How come this fellow only makes his presence known after a month?

He finishes his coffee. His brow is really furrowed. It's because, I tell him, it's in the terms of the contract for the ad to appear every three weeks. It's actually just been reprinted. Then, having thought for a while: But maybe it's also because people are starting to talk about me and I'm now known. Maybe I'm gaining a reputation in this little town.

I call Françoise. I think it will be useful to discuss the letter from this man with her. She can tell me how she reacts to it as a woman. After all, this whole idea was hers in the first place. She dragged me into this adventure so she needs to take some responsibility. She needs to know where I've got to. And to give me her advice.

We meet at the Black Radish, a vegetarian restaurant she loves. She's ordered her usual, creamed barley with radishes (the house speciality), which she apparently finds irresistible. I've chosen a cold tomato soup. I tell her everything. She seems stunned by Eric's story, but is enthusiastic about the rest. She feels it all sounds very good, very promising. She thinks her idea was brilliant, that I'm on the road to success and will soon be earning my living. On condition, she says, changing tack slightly between two spoonfuls of her creamed barley, that I avoid more careless mistakes. The one I made with Eric was major. As far as the 'gentleman' is concerned, she does wonder, she's not too sure, we'll have to see… I tell her that we definitely will see, but I can't just let something like this, such an opportunity, pass me by. Yes, she says, of course, but it's important to find out what sort of man he is… A managing director, fine, but… I can see where he's coming from, this man of yours. I ask her whether, in my shoes, she would go to see him. Yes, she'd go. Either way, she says, you're grown up enough to judge…

She starts gazing up at the ceiling, closing her eyes, dreaming. You're grown up enough, Marie-Constance, and yet you're still the wonderful girl you were at eighteen. A funny thing you are too. But wonderful and unforgettable. She keeps her eyes closed, as if lost in the depths of memory. Do you remember when we did *Waiting for Godot*? I can't really remember if it was before or after the Conservatoire. I seem to think it was before. We played Pozzo and Lucky – I was Pozzo, you were Lucky. Four of us had decided to put the play on together with girls in every role: Clotilde played Vladimir and Laurence was Estragon. They already had a bit of experience... we were just beginners. We settled for the minor roles, that's right. I was Pozzo and you were Lucky... I was holding you on a sort of halter, a rope that went round your neck, do you remember? You were very funny in that role, fantastic. A completely non-speaking part, since we had decided to cut Lucky's monologue, which was a shame because your voice is so lovely, so warm, so captivating. But we didn't really know about your voice back then, didn't really appreciate it...

And is it any better appreciated now? I can see myself as I was then, on the skinny side, even around the buttocks in those days, with that slip knot round my neck, wearing an old potato sack, barefoot, with Françoise tugging the end of the rope, me sticking my tongue out... I did very well with comedy material. Now I'm engaged with more serious stuff. Countesses, managing directors. I wonder what Françoise really thinks. If she were me (I ask again) would she give this letter a positive reply? Positive... positive... she ponders. I don't know! But I'd go and have a look, for sure, at least to find out what the guy looks like... Beyond that, I've already told you what I think. I don't have much experience, but I can tell you...

She tells me something I've already heard a hundred times. When she first went to work for the lawyer, Maître Blanc, she was basically just a little typist who wanted a job, the quickest and easiest, something you could get with minimal qualifications. Then she gradually reached the point where she'd secured the lawyer's trust and took direct responsibility for some of his work, until she really was a director's personal assistant, most likely because she was proactive, efficient and conscientious too, impeccably conscientious about her work, qualities for which she was recognized... Until the day (and here her face takes on a sort of glow of pathos)... until the day when Maître Blanc's practice had achieved some status and he saw fit to take on an associate, Maître Bonnet... and disaster struck... Constant sexual harassment... Actually, what do I mean harassment? It was blackmail. Yes, blackmail. I thought everything was falling apart, going under... I thought I'd have to leave, my job had had it... Well, says Françoise, I stood my ground.

She breaks off for a moment to order a low-fat yoghurt. She pins me with her huge tragic eyes, clutches my wrist. Yes, I stood my ground... I got things straight once and for all with Maître Bonnet. By being not aggressive, but firm. That's how you have to handle things with men. Not only did I save my job, but I saved the Blanc–Bonnet practice. The most successful in town. And not only does Bonnet now respect me, but he recognizes that I'm his most reliable colleague. We're friends, good friends. That's men for you. It's quite simple. Yes, quite simple, I say stupidly. And I order a low-fat yoghurt too.

Another session with Eric. As usual there's the inevitable fifteen-minute conversation with his mother before I start. She certainly does like aprons: she's wearing a very pretty one today, small and mauve-coloured. Out of the blue and apparently for no particular reason, Eric starts talking about cats in front of her. He's passionate about cats. He'd like to have one. His mother refuses point blank, saying that all the doctors who look after him have said he's allergic to cat hair and if he touches it or inhales it he could have an asthma attack or a violent, spasmodic nervous reaction. You remember, don't you? his mother says. You've seen him and we're not going through that again for a cat! The boy doesn't appear to see things in the same way at all. He says it isn't true, it's a fabrication, that they're just trying to stop him having a cat. He puts on a performance, raging and crying, contorting himself in his chrome wheelchair. He suddenly looks like a toddler, a ridiculous toddler throwing a tantrum.

I ask him what inspired this love of cats. He instantly stops grimacing, changes his expression, his whole face and tone of voice, and says: Baudelaire did. It's difficult to disguise my surprise. His mother looks dumbstruck. He explains calmly that he found a copy of *The Flowers of Evil* in the library of the institution he attends three days a week. He read it, he didn't completely understand everything but really loved some of the poems. Like the one called 'Cats'. He recites a few lines from memory:

> *Powerful yet gentle cats,*
> *The pride of the household,*
> *Shying from the cold as they do*
> *And just as sedentary...*

He speaks in one breath, in a rush, with something utterly smooth and clear about his voice. I think of how I myself intoned Baudelaire not that long ago in the echo chamber. His voice, as a strange echo of my own. He certainly doesn't lack sensitivity, or talent even. His mother, who clearly knows nothing of this talent, looks astonished and is dumbstruck. After a moment, though, she regains the power of speech and asks Eric whether he's brought home the book he's just mentioned. Yes, he says, and, turning the wheels of his chair with swift thrusts of his palms, he rolls out of the room, heads for his bedroom and comes back at the same speed, still pushing his wheels and threading his way around the furniture as if paddling between reefs, bringing with him the book, a classic edition, which he brandishes like a trophy. *The Flowers of Evil!* exclaims his mother, with no other comment. She takes the book from Eric's hand, slaps it on the table and, as if governed by an irresistible impulse, grabs the wheelchair and, pushing it even more quickly than her son did, takes him to his bedroom, shuts him in and locks the door with a turn of the key.

Ashen-faced, she comes back over to me, picks up the book, shows it to me and says: You see? Did you hear that?

Do you understand? Do you think Eric can read this book at his age? Her fingers are shaking as she clutches the book. I take time formulating a reply. And deliver it as coolly, as serenely, as possible: Yes, I think he can. She looks relieved. She clearly trusts me. I have the rather pleasant impression that we've almost toppled into another laughable melodrama but have escaped just in time. Unless, back in his room, Eric's having a fit as we speak. And actually, in a way, he has reason enough. He's really being treated like a little boy. I listen out. Is he ranting? Is he crying? No. Silence. Go and get him, I tell his mother. She complies, sheepish and embarrassed. She unlocks the bedroom door and wheels the chair back out. Eric is very calm, almost indifferent. Gazing around him. In order to settle the matter and break the tension once and for all, I turn to him and say: You're right, Baudelaire's a great poet, and a great cat lover... That's exactly what we're going to read today, his poem 'Cats', and perhaps some others... The idea just came to me from nowhere. It must be a good one, because Eric is beaming. His mother seems to be beaming too. She leaves us together and we go off to his bedroom, where the reading session begins.

We go back to Baudelaire's 'Cats':

> *Devotees of learning and*
> *voluptuous pleasure,*
> *They seek out the silence and horror*
> *of darkest night...*

Eric is listening very attentively, with a sort of contained passion. I'm oddly transported by my own voice too and, as

I read, I feel as if the poem is an extraordinary mechanism, a fantastical clockwork machine, and all its component parts, its every articulation, could be laid bare, if that was what I wanted, if I took the trouble, if I was still up to those textual analyses that I handled pretty well at school, or so they said, so they assured me, so they insisted, promising me a future I've never had, given that I'm here now, reduced to the pathetic position of reader-cum-sick nurse. Pathetic, no. Bathetic. Just modest, very modest. But, at the end of the day, not actually as modest as that, because I do seem to be making someone happy right now.

Eric's feverish attention really is growing increasingly intense. We carry on to the end of the poem. I say *we* because, although I'm the only one reading, I can tell that the two of us are very much sharing something. And that's just as it should be. Now we've reached the end of the piece, I look up at Eric. But he doesn't even give me time to catch my breath. He's rolled his wheelchair over to me, taken the book from my hand and is leafing through it hurriedly, as if he knows every inch of every page. He opens it to a particular poem, which he points out to me, then hands the book back, saying: What about reading this one? This one? It's the one called 'Jewels'. I don't remember it very well. I glance through it quickly: it's beautiful, but risqué. Something of it hovers in the back of my mind, a half-memory, not so much because of Baudelaire, I admit, but a song – by which I mean a musical setting – that someone must have made of it. I've forgotten exactly who, Ferré or Montand, more likely Montand; I can hear the characteristic inflections of his voice, warm, soft and smooth… It's actually one of the most famous of Baudelaire's 'condemned poems'. Eric has chosen well. He has good taste, good intuition; he certainly is a special case.

Should I read it? I hesitate for a moment, then make up my mind:

My beloved was naked and, knowing my desire,
Wore nothing on her person but her tinkling jewels.
Thus richly attired, she had the grace and fire
Of Moorish slave girls on high days and holidays…

Eric is now even more attentive. He looks utterly spellbound, not missing one word of the poem. And he glances down at my legs – in trousers again today – with that strange furtive movement he manages to make with his eyes. I carry on reading slowly, right up to the famous verse:

Her arm, her leg, her loins and her thighs,
Shiny as oil and sinuous as a swan,
Paraded before my serene, receptive eyes…

At this point Eric interrupts me and, in the silence of that shadowy sick room with its drawn curtains, he says: Next time, couldn't you come in the dress from the other day, please?

The temperature has changed. The season is marching on. It's still a sunny autumn but there's already that tobacco colour stealing over everything, from trees to buildings, proving that we're tipping towards winter. The pavement I'm walking on is ash grey. I'm wearing a pair of soft, supple boots that I'm comfortable in for my visit to La Générale. The second visit. I'm not filled with excessive enthusiasm, I have to admit. But duty calls.

The unavoidable maid greets me even more starchily than last time, and shows me into a sitting room I haven't yet had the privilege of seeing. Madame is asleep, she says, you'll have to wait a moment. It strikes me that La Générale sleeps a lot. And here I am bang on time: three o'clock in the afternoon, on the agreed day, Tuesday. Would you like some orange tea? the maid asks in a steely voice. That's when I notice the peculiar coincidence that she too is wearing boots. But hers are completely different from mine. First, because they're being worn indoors, which is slightly surprising. Then because they're not supple at all but rather stiff-looking, buttoned right up and austerely black. Besides, they're partly hidden by a long leather skirt which is even more unusual-looking. The strange character is also wearing a blouse (is it the same as last time?) that's tight enough around her neck to strangle her. And her hair is raked into a severe bun. I thank her, say I'll have some tea later, if she really insists. She seems to think that my unfortunate wording, 'if you really insist', has a very unpleasant ring to it. She looks offended but also saddened, pained. As I sit down in an armchair, she brazenly sits herself bang opposite me and starts watching me in silence, as if trying to communicate some unspoken reproach.

I wonder whether this will go on long. And it does seem to go on. There is a large nineteenth-century clock to my right. I look at it, as if asking for help. But the two long metal hands look depressingly immobile. She's immobile too, sitting there so upright, facing me, and watching me in that pointed way that all of a sudden appears to slip into something almost affectionate. The seconds pass. I let my eyes rove around the room, in order not to confront hers. The walls are full of souvenirs and old paintings. In a frame hang military decorations, medals, a wide sash with a sort of imperial eagle. Navigation charts, prints. Dusty museum pieces. But in the corner over there stands a small display cabinet that looks a bit more spruce, caught in the beams of two electric lights, as if they were spotlights. How curious. I stand to have a look, an opportunity to break up this oppressive one-to-one. The cabinet is filled with little red flags imprinted with the hammer and sickle; one of them is pierced, shredded, as if lacerated by bullets. There are also all sorts of insignia and engravings, presumably of revolutionary incidents, various scenes from the Paris Commune, two large pictures with primary colours like tarot cards depicting historical characters with their names inscribed above them: if I'm reading correctly (but I have to lean forward to see), Matthias Corvinus Rex and (really very tricky to decipher) Béla Kun. Above the cabinet there is a photograph of Lenin on a stand designed to look like a sheaf of corn and topped with a red star. The two spotlights are illuminating this photo, like a pair of tapers on an altar.

That's Madame's special corner, the knife-edged voice tells me. Then, after a huge sigh: What a waste of electricity! She has to have it lit up the whole time. I carry on peering, leaning forward, my hands behind my back. Another sigh. It's a complete craze of Madame's, she goes on, an affliction. She'll never be cured of it now. She's even said she'll disinherit her entire family if they don't take her seriously. Third sigh. Of course we have to take her seriously, but it causes such consternation. No one comes to see her any more, and I have to put up with everything. For how long? She'll end up all alone and completely mad. Well, you've already seen that for yourself! I reply without turning round: I haven't seen anything. She's charming and full of energy for her age, remarkably lucid. Searing retort: Well, you'd better go and see her, then!

At that exact moment a bell rings. La Générale calls from her bedroom. She must have noticed that she's missed our appointment. I find her sitting up in bed with a huge pillow behind her, looking perfectly refreshed and sparkly-eyed. Nouchka, she says, reaching her hand towards me, I've slept a little longer than I meant to. Forgive me, but I'm ready now. We can carry on reading exactly where we left off. Just let me throw a shawl over my shoulders, or actually you could help me do it. I help her cover herself with a large red woollen shawl. Wonderful, gorgeous colour! she says with an impressive Magyar roll. She sits back comfortably. There, off we go! She hands me the book, with a marker on the page where I had to stop last time. I have no choice. I have to carry on with this awful passage:

From the time when the private ownership of movable objects developed, all companies that recognized such ownership had to comply with the commonly held moral commandment: Thou shalt not steal…

She interrupts me with a snigger: Thou shalt not steal! And how! That's all they did all their lives, those boyars, they stole from the people! Carry on, Nouchka.

But did this commandment thereby become an everlasting moral commandment? Not in any sense. In a society in which there is no longer any motivation for theft, where eventually thefts would therefore be committed only by the insane, how laughable seems the moralizing preacher who tries solemnly to pronounce this eternal truth: Thou shalt not steal!

Yes, she says, interrupting me again, laughable! The insane, there would be no one left to steal but the insane! That's true genius! Don't you think, Nouchka? But I think you're finding this boring… Put the book down and take this one, here… It's *The Critique of Political Economy*… I'm sure you think Marx only wrote excruciatingly boring things. It's clear from your expression and the slightly disgusted way you read… Well, think again. Have a look at this passage, the one on the page with the tortoiseshell bookmark – it must be page 166… You'll see, it's a wonderful piece about precious metals... It could have been written by a poet... wouldn't you say?... Well, read on.

I open the book at the indicated page. I'm very irritated, tense even, and it must show. I still read, though. This passage is marked with a cross too:

> *Gold and silver do not display the negative character-istics of superfluity, are not dispensable: their aesthetic qualities make them naturally appropriate to pomp, adornment and sumptuousness, prerequisites for feast days and holidays; they are, in a sense, the positive form of all things superfluous and luxurious...*

She gestures for me to stop and asks: What do you say to that, Nouchka? *Pomp, adornment and sumptuousness? Prerequisites for feast days?* Be honest. Tell me you weren't expecting that!... I'm wondering what on earth to say to her, how to reply, when I hear the door open slowly. I turn around, thinking it's that other *creature* bringing her tea. But it isn't. It's the mauve cat. The door can't have been completely closed and he's pushed it open with his neck and his arched back. He pads into the room and, without a moment's hesitation, jumps on to the bed. The countess takes him in her arms and starts stroking him, meanwhile indicating (rather emphatically) that I should carry on. Which I do:

> *They are to some extent like light in its pristine purity, extracted from the underworld by man; since silver reflects all the light rays in the spectrum in their original*

*combination, and gold reflects only red, the most potent
of colours...*

Do you hear that? she says. (No, I can't hear anything. I've
said I find it hard hearing the sound of my own voice, and
that's certainly not going to change here with her!) Do you
hear that? *Light in its pristine purity! Gold reflects only red,
the most potent of colours!* Red! Is there any better way
of putting it! It's so beautiful! She closes her eyes, literally
swooning, still stroking the cat.

*A sense of colour is in fact the most widespread form
of aesthetic appreciation in general. The etymological
similarities in various Indo-European languages linking
the names of precious metals and expressions of colour
were established by Jacob Grimm...*

In such a swoon, with her eyes so tightly closed that I
wonder whether she hasn't drifted off to sleep again. And
the cat too.

I've put on a pair of glasses and a nicely tailored jacket.

I've made up my mind. I'm off to see my managing director. His name is Michel Dautrand. We arranged the appointment by telephone. Six o'clock in the evening: a respectable time. As I walk into the achingly modern building where he lives – the Résidence Ravel – I'm clearly not coming to see just anyone. Such luxury and elegance. The lift shaft is made entirely of glass: a cylinder of smoked glass through which you can look down on to the building's closely mown lawns. Even this late in the year they look perfectly green and fresh.

The gentleman who opens the door to me is well groomed, distinguished, still young, not bad. Still young: this means he must be between forty and fifty, let's say forty-five, if I've got my eye in. Not bad: like a rather tired John Wayne, unless I'm deluding myself. But this John Wayne isn't easy company at all. From our first exchange he seems curt, strict, stiff, straight. Mademoiselle, he says, offering me a magnificent white leather pouffe, here's the thing. I have extremely demanding responsibilities in this town, where my company has set up its head office. Here and elsewhere in fact, because I travel a great deal, and I don't have a moment to myself to read anything at all. Now, for the purposes of my job, I attend a good many important dinners where the conversation covers everything, and very frequently literature, by which I mean contemporary literature, and because I'd rather not always look like an idiot or illiterate, I thought that with your help, Mademoiselle... Having had no opportunity to interrupt because he's spoken this without drawing breath, I break in suddenly now, as curt as he is: It's Madame. He doesn't seem to understand, looks rather thrown. It's not Mademoiselle, it's Madame, I say again. Ah, he says, yes... Ah, yes...

I can tell he's going to find it hard to pick up the thread. In fact, he seems to have given up on unravelling his long sentence and asks whether I'd like something to drink. Perhaps a small whisky, I say, thinking this will make a change from tea and coffee. He looks rather surprised but tries not to show it. He goes over to a beautiful sideboard in Scandinavian pine to fetch a bottle of Famous Grouse and two glasses. He pours mine. Is that all right? he asks. A little more, I say. He looks up at me, eyeing me with obvious concern. He pours some more (too much this time). Pours himself some. Asks whether I'd like ice. I don't want any. He does, though. He fetches it. Swirls the ice cubes in his glass. Yes, he says... (but his voice is one degree deeper), yes... my life's too busy... you know, with business... particularly a business like mine... I deal with metals... Even as a tiny child I dreamed of metals. I adored them... seeing them, touching them... In a way I've succeeded, I've done what I wanted to do... I extract metals from the earth and import them... You see what I mean, mining...

I raise my glass to eye level, as if drinking his health, and say: So are you digging things up from the earth locally? Our mines are pretty much all over the world, he says, particularly in New Caledonia. Nickel... But I'm sure I don't need to draw you a picture of New Caledonia. You see what I'm talking about... and I don't know whether we'll be able to carry on with the nickel for very long... Luckily we have mines in Africa too, major mines... Just tilting my drink to my lips, I say I can now see why he travels. Ah, he says, yes, I do travel, planes, airports, the awful jet set... but also trains, the high-speed TGV quite a lot, to get to Paris... I'm beginning to wonder why he doesn't have time to read if he's often on the TGV or a plane. I ask him. Oh well, Madame, he says, of course I read on journeys, but files, always work files!

I can just see him with his attaché case, or his overflowing briefcase, or his elegant suitcase, dashing from stations to airports. Like all the rest of them, fretting, hurrying. Trying to look important. In a shower of expenses receipts. His company! His nickel! And not the tiniest window in his schedule to read a book. But then how does he have time for *me*? For the time I'm supposed to be devoting to his education? The answer is very simple, very straightforward, almost certainly rehearsed, premeditated: Listen, Madame, I'm going to admit something to you. It's not just about time. I'm incapable, do you hear me, *incapable* of reading books. It must be something to do with my schooling, my way of life, the constant bustle of my work. I don't know, but that's the way it is... But, if someone could give me... a bit of help... If a *voice*, and it may well be yours, helped me... give me access to books... Do you see what I mean? I tell him there are cassettes, good-quality recordings that he could listen to on the train, in the plane, on a boat, and there are also all sorts of speed-reading techniques perfected specifically for overstretched businessmen. He looks sheepish, wounded, contrite: You don't understand... I'm trying to explain that this needs to be... How can I put this?... Personalized... His tone of voice suddenly changes and he gets to his feet as if no longer wanting to sit there facing me: Right then, are you prepared to provide the service that your advertisement implies you offer? I'd be delighted if you were. Actually, the trickiest part will be timetabling it because of my schedule, but your terms...

I interrupt him with a wave of my hand. In the ensuing silence I let my eyes rove around the room, which feels huge and empty despite the beautiful reproductions (or perhaps they're originals) of modern paintings gracing the walls. In fact, the whole apartment feels huge and empty. Does he live alone? He wears a wedding ring. And your wife? I ask. He looks piqued: I'm sorry... my wife? Can't she read to you? I feel as if I've struck him some sort of blow. He instantly drops back down on to the pouffe where he'd been sitting, opposite mine. He hangs his head, takes his forehead in his hands, then looks up: his hair is all mussed up and his features express pure helplessness. The managing director has been reduced to a kind of pitiful puppet. As if to complete the picture, he loosens the knot of his tie and unbuttons his collar. We separated, he says, more than a year ago... Please believe me... I live all alone... He says it again: *all alone*... not even a cleaner... Actually, yes, a cleaner from work, that's all... And, I say, is that why you'd like to be read to?

When I leave I promise to think it over. At least to send him my little brochure. His whole bearing has changed. He takes my hand beseechingly. What should I read, he asks, Duras? That may not be enough, you know, I tell him. People are talking about Claude Simon for the Nobel and, if that does happen, there'll be a lot of discussion about him at dinners. But I warn you, it's not easy. He holds on to my hand. I wonder whether he'll ever let go. Come back, he says. Come back soon.

I comply with Eric's wishes. I arrive wrapped head to toe in a long raincoat – it's been raining doggedly since yesterday – and that's how his mother finds me on the doorstep (Let's take that off, put your umbrella down, get you dry!). Once in the bedroom for the reading session, I'm back in my crêpe dress over bare legs as if it were high summer (and she's had time to notice, to clock this anomaly and give a brief frown).

Eric immediately shows how pleased he is. He seems eager, impatient. His features are peculiarly mobile. Right, he says, let's read. My hair's still wet but I sit down in the usual chair, making the fabric of my dress billow in my lap, and start another Maupassant story, because despite the Baudelaire interlude he wants us to stick to Maupassant, saying that he enjoys his books, finds them really entertaining, just what he feels like (and in this obstinacy there is probably an element of determination to show that his outburst that first time has done nothing to put him off fantastical or supernatural stories). This is a story about a group of men who gather one windy evening to go shooting:

A great wind was howling outside, an autumn wind, roaring and galloping, one of those winds that kills the last of the leaves and carries them off into the clouds...

As I read I let my dead-leaf dress rise up my thighs, very gradually and as if it were happening naturally. He watches. I can hear his breathing quite distinctly. Mine becomes fast, halting. I'm finding it really difficult to carry on reading, to enunciate properly. But I must:

The men were just finishing their supper, still booted, ruddy-faced, buzzing, excited…

I've no idea what I'm reading. I've no idea what this story is about. Just the words. To think I can never usually hear what I'm saying, but this time I distinctly hear the words I'm reading:… *still booted, ruddy-faced, buzzing, excited…*

Eric is very calm. He's never seemed more attentive to the story. His breathing, which is regular but getting deeper and deeper, is a gauge of his concentration. I think that his eyes, lowered towards me, are attentive too. I raise my dress further. Pull it almost to the top of my thighs. I don't know what sort of wild wind is blowing inside my head. Nor in his. I can't control a slight quivering in my knees, or in my hands as they hold the book. He can see me perfectly clearly. He's listening. Time goes by. The story, the words go by. This shooting party, it turns out, is made up of *the demi-lords of Normandy, men who were half country squire, half peasant, wealthy and muscular, built to break the horns off an ox… they bellowed when they talked…* I can't hear a thing: *They bellowed when they talked.* It's hot in this draught-proof room, so hot that I'm wondering whether I didn't actually do the right thing wearing this dress. But the rain's still coming down outside. Which poet was it who said it comes down 'thick and bland'? I mustn't forget that Eric likes poetry too, and should be introduced to more of it. We're not going to become full-time subscribers to Maupassant! But we're there now, the story has resolved into a leisurely rhythm. Here we go with the shooting party! I manage to control my breathing a bit. And Eric's is slowing, settling. We're both very calm.

The door opens. Eric's mother (did she knock?) brings in hot chocolate. I just have time to pull my dress back down, pronto.

At La Générale's house today I have to wait till I'm summoned again. Even though I'm bang on time. In the living-room-museum I once again have the difficult task of sitting facing *her*, the maid, the *creature*, less buttoned up than last time, but apparently still as keen to keep me company.

Just to have something to say, I comment on how odd it is that the display cabinet should be lit the whole time. Why doesn't she turn those spotlights off? Even if La Générale is obsessive and insistent about it, she can't check what's going on from her bed. Oh, she says, you don't know her. She gets up! Seeing my slight amazement, she explains that the countess (she doesn't say La Générale when referring to her employer, but the countess) is not at all incapacitated, despite what her lengthy interludes in bed might imply, absolutely not. Her habit of staying in bed is just a way of conserving her strength and making allowances for – or, more precisely, forcing others to make allowances for – her great age, but sometimes she throws off the covers when you least expect it, gets out of bed, bends down to pick up the walking stick that she keeps hidden under the bed, and prowls, stick in hand, all round the apartment, having put on a dressing gown, of course.

You don't know her! she says again. This is so she can inspect everything. If you only knew what she puts me through sometimes! And the humiliations! (Rudimentary sniffling, false tears held in check.) Here's an example: I'm sure you'll agree *I* could have been her reader, I like books and my voice is no more unpleasant than anyone else's (oh, but it is, steely voice!), well, she gets *you* to come here, she chooses you! To humiliate me, do you see, to humiliate me.

Suddenly realizing that she's genuinely unhappy and mortified, or at least I think she is, I tell her there's no privilege in reading Marx, it's actually more of a dreadful chore, that she should be counting her blessings for avoiding it. I don't know who this Marx is, she retorts tartly, but what I do know is that her whole family view it as a shame and a curse, at her age, don't you see, that sort of book! The sniffling and false tears are back. I opt not to say anything in the face of this exasperating play-acting. Probably realizing that I'm irritated, she moves her chair closer to mine and says: Whatever you do, don't go thinking I'm jealous of you or of your position. I know you're much more capable than I am… more cultured… I know your voice is much nicer (deep sigh)… but also you're much more attractive (I should hope so!)… Yes, you're really very pretty (extra deep sigh).

La Générale herself comes and extricates me from this awkward situation. As if she can hear the conversation through the wall and wants to give a sort of instant illustration of what her housekeeper's been saying, she sweeps into the room with her walking stick, oddly draped in her dressing gown, half actress, half ghost, obviously broken by old age but still formidable, theatrical in spite of herself. Nouchka, she says, there you are. Come, let me take your arm. And now she's showing me all around the room, tethered to my arm. The creature has disappeared in a flash. The walking stick bangs down on the floorboards with imperious regularity. It's as if La Générale wants to mark out all the stations of some cross, some pilgrimage. And we do actually have to stop at every engraving, every painting, every ornament. That, she says, is the coat of arms of the Austro-Hungarian Empire – I'm sure you recognize the two-headed eagle – and this is the sash of the Order of the Regency, with which my husband was decorated. There's no point my telling you that I don't attach the least importance to these trinkets from a bygone age. I keep them here out of respect for his memory, but to balance things out, here, kept under glass, I have the first petition – look, it's handwritten – by the poor Ukrainian peasants of the Carpathians. It's a document that never fails to move me. Can you see the blood, the tears that soaked into the paper?... Come, Nouchka! Hobbling, stamping with her walking stick and leaning heavily on my arm, she trails me over to the glass cabinet, and here she looks triumphant and seems to breathe more freely. As you can see, she says, this is a completely different matter, a different world, a different light! That's why I keep the electricity on day and night, even though my family think it an outrage (spectacular rolling of that 'r'). They're so middle class, miserly as little shopkeepers who can think of nothing better to do than count their money, by which I mean watch their precious bank balance. They just don't understand that the world is *changing gear*... Do you see what I mean, Nouchka?... Anyway, I don't need to explain this cabinet to you, it speaks for itself... If you'd like one of these little badges for the lapel of your jacket, if you ever wear a jacket, that is, I could give you one of them. The choice is yours… but I really want you to have a look at this flag, which was torn by bullets on the barricades at Pest in '46 and which probably still smells of gunpowder… And also the photo there… No, not the one of Vladimir Ilyich… No, the little one, at the bottom… A unique document… and I won't tell you how it came into my possession, Nouchka. Have a look… she taps the end of her walking stick on the glass with something like impatience, pointing to a yellowed photo in the corner on the first shelf. On it I can make out a young man praying. She leans towards my ear and whispers: Stalin, Nouchka, when he was a seminarian in Georgia.

Then she takes my arm again and leads me off to her bedroom: Now let's go and read!

It's winter. But the sun is resplendent. I meet Roland Sora in a park near the university. He felt like stretching his legs outside. I've put on a thick woollen jacket over ski pants. He's wearing an old fur-lined jacket that looks just the thing with his pipe. To our right, naked trees. But on the left, a line of privet in a tenacious green. There are children playing on slides and swings.

I tell him about my managing director. More specifically I say I'm planning to read him some Claude Simon, to complete his education to the highest level, so that during his business dinners he really can have the best of intellectual profiles. My 'old master' wonders whether I haven't gone completely mad this time. He takes my arm in that slightly condescending way people use with someone who needs careful handling, who mustn't be rushed. I leave him in no doubt that I'm very clear about my intentions and that, aware of my mission as a reader and the decisive effect it could now have in some cases, I want to strive not for mediocrity but for excellence. I might as well aim for the top. He doesn't respond to this but takes me over to a slide where a very small girl preparing to go down the chute gathers up her skirt as we come towards her. He looks at her and smiles, in a sort of dream. I go back to what I was saying: Yes, I'll start with a few pages of *The Flanders Road...* or perhaps *The Georgics...* Without taking his eyes off the little girl and talking absently, as if to himself, he says: Yes, that's very you, my irreplaceable and brilliantly cultured Marie-Constance (honestly, such a shame you never finished your studies), but believe me, if you really want to go with Claude Simon, that's not where you should start, particularly with a managing director. What you need is *Lesson in Things*… As the title implies, there's an element of some sort of *lesson* in it, but there are also simple realities, or *things*… You couldn't ask for better for a beginner.

Of course I'm aware of the utterly condescending but also slightly bitter irony in these last words. But he's not a beginner, I retort, he's cultivated, charismatic, refined, commanding, a very fine figure of a man too. He's read a great deal, but he wants to keep up to date, that's all, because he's so busy now he doesn't have time to read. Good, Roland Sora says, perfect! And he's relying on you for this? Well, yes, I say, on me. He took my ad seriously, took my work seriously!

The master takes me over to an empty bench at the far end of the park. How about sitting in the sun for a bit? he says. I say it's a good idea, but that it's actually getting quite cold and we won't be able to stay long. We've barely sat down when an old woman comes and settles herself on the same bench, right at the end. She's holding a daisy that she must have picked but I can't think where. You'd think she's come to listen to what we're saying. Roland looks irritated. He leans towards my ear – I can feel his warm, gentle breath on my lobe – and he murmurs: So, as far as I can make out, it's going OK, it's working. What's working? I reply inanely. He leans a little closer, as if he really doesn't want anyone to hear: It's working with this new client… working well… at the highest level? I get the feeling he's making fun of me, so I reply: He's not a client, he's already a friend, a very distinguished man, as it happens. The old woman isn't paying the least attention to what we're saying. She's brought the daisy up to her face and starts pulling its petals out conscientiously. Well, I'm conscientious too.

I've been back to see the man at the agency to ask him to run my ad again, because under the terms of my contract it stops being rerun automatically after a specific period. He looked surprised. He was still chewing on his cigarette butt. He still eyed me with the same perplexed expression. I told him things were going well, but he didn't seem to believe me. A combination of perfect scepticism and bovine indifference. His way of implying: None of this is any of my business… If you're happy with it, well fine… If you have any problems, don't come running to me… He asked me whether I wanted to keep the same wording. I hesitated, then asked him to add 'poetry'. Instead of 'Young woman available to read to you in your own home. Works of literature, non-fiction, any sort of book you like', I want to say: 'Young woman available to read to you in your own home. Works of literature, non-fiction, poetry, any sort of book you like.' One extra word: ten extra francs. A little luxury. He made it clear he thought this ridiculous. That having 'poetry' sent the whole ad reeling into absurdity. I held my ground. A minor act of defiance, but it mattered to me.

And the result wasn't long in coming. A young woman from the upper echelons of local society has written asking me whether I could read 'poetry' to her eight-year-old daughter from time to time. I'm now with this woman. Listening to her. She's extremely beautiful, elegant and well turned out. These are her concerns: she works, she's a property developer, she doesn't have a spare minute and is quite unable to look after her little girl. She needs someone dedicated to do it for her. I tell her that I'm not a private tutor but a *reader*, she must have misunderstood. She keeps me there with a dazzling smile. Not at all, she saw exactly what the ad meant, she hasn't misunderstood anything, if I would just let her make the point she wants to make: she could have as many private tutors as she likes, if that's what was needed, but the child works hard at school, that isn't the problem, the problem is that she's alone when she's home, sometimes for long evenings, and she desperately needs someone to entertain her and stimulate her mind at the same time, and… perhaps even show her a little tenderness that she, being such a busy woman, is – alas – not always able to give the child… She's looking me right in the eye, as if really hoping to persuade; her beautiful film-star face has an almost pathetic gorgeousness to it with its immaculate hairdo, its spectacular blue eyelids, magnificently defined eyelashes, turquoise earrings, matching necklace, and that authority in her eyes and in her voice. There's nothing more dreadful, she says, than being a working mother… Stay-at-home mothers who bemoan their situation don't know how lucky they are… living their lives at a peaceful pace, being able to devote themselves to their children… We're completely thwarted in that respect… Even more so for those of us with lots of responsibilities like myself; I don't even have time to catch my breath… and with a husband abroad… But I will say one thing: I couldn't for a moment imagine giving up this manic lifestyle and my responsibilities… They're my destiny, my lot in life… I can't picture myself any other way... Can't imagine a different life for myself... And it keeps getting worse, getting more intense, accumulating all the time... Some of my friends even say I should go into politics... Perhaps I'm made for it... Either way, I'm happy living like this, in this whirlwind, this madness... and that's why there's this terrible problem and I'm asking you to help me resolve it... Clorinde, you'll soon see, is very sweet, very endearing... If you'll allow me, I'll go and get her...

Is this going to be a replay of Eric's mother? I ask myself, feeling slightly uncomfortable. Granted, this woman is completely different, she's actually more like my managing director. But that's exactly what's bothering me: a sudden juxtaposition, a mixing of the two situations. Managing-director-lady and mummy-lady. As it happens, Clorinde *is* indisputably sweet. When she comes in with her mother, I'm instantly charmed by her fresh little face framed by curly hair. A pointy nose. A dusting of freckles on her cheeks. A mischievous, intelligent expression. But I immediately find myself wondering what on earth I can do for a child like her. I certainly hadn't anticipated dealing with eight-year-olds. What should I read to her? *Alice's Adventures in Wonderland*?

I must have thought out loud. That's right, the mother says, *Alice's Adventures in Wonderland*, exactly right. She's never read it and I think it's just the book she needs, a book that will give her imagination free rein and introduce her to poetry... because I want her to be introduced to poetry... Business is like a drug to me, you see... I'm always buzzing around, travelling, having lunches left, right and centre... For her, something different, the essentials, poetry... You've got it just right and you've chosen just right... Clorinde doesn't say a word. She must be intimidated, but every now and then she looks up at me with her clear eyes, as if checking what she's got to deal with. The smallest of smiles is developing on her lips. She must like me. And I like her too. You see, I really do come up against the most unpredictable situations. But this one certainly isn't the most unpleasant. Or the most difficult, come to think of it. It's a deal. I agree to it. I'm not sure, I tell the mummy-businesswoman, that I'm best equipped to look after a child Clorinde's age – I certainly don't have the necessary qualifications or any special training – but if this is what she wants, and if Clorinde wants it too, if we're all in agreement, if it's clear no one's expecting me to do more than read, I'm happy to give it a try. Clorinde looks up again and this time she gives a nod of approval. Yes, she wants this.

At home that evening I dig out an old copy of *Alice*, and while I wait for Philippe, who usually gets home late, I set about reading a few lines at random in the echo chamber. It's the part where the White Rabbit has lost his fan and kid gloves, and asks Alice to fetch them for him. She looks all around the great hall, under the glass table, and realizes he's taken her for his housemaid. I say the sentence again in the cocoon-like silence of the room: *He took me for his housemaid*. I think Clorinde's mother might also have taken me for her housemaid. Like La Générale. Like all of them. Perhaps. Can't be sure. I have to accept the constraints of the job, and its risks. In any event, I have a proper clientele now. I even have a little girl, me who's never had a little girl or a little boy. On the left-hand page of the book, where I've left it open, there's a beautiful cross-hatched pen and ink illustration of the Rabbit with his fan and his gloves, and Alice in a strange diaphanous dress. And on the right-hand page a photograph of the Reverend Charles Dodgson, who so liked photographing little girls himself.

Having decided to pursue the experiment with Michel Dautrand, I'm heading for his apartment with a Claude Simon book. I've kept the glasses, but abandoned the tailored jacket. The preppy look is over. I've gone all out for velvet trousers. It has to be said, I might as well choose clothes that are going to protect me. I hope this customer won't be as disappointed as Eric. I'll know from the look on his face.

It's funny, because he's been through more or less the same thought process as me. He's abandoned the jacket and tie. He's wearing a big shapeless sweater and looks very relaxed, a lot more than last time at any rate. He tells me straight away that he only has an hour to spare and not two as planned. So I'll have to do some 'intensive reading' (that's the expression he uses). This is probably why he drops down into a large armchair, crosses his hands behind his neck, closes his eyes and waits. I'm invited to take another armchair. But I choose the pouffe. I explain briefly that Claude Simon should provide 'intensive reading' because his work is very dense. But I add that he shouldn't hope for a story, for events and anecdotes: just beautiful writing where every word in the text has its own weight. I've chosen a passage from *Lesson in Things* which describes a painting or engraving:

Three women who probably have delicate complexions, because they are protecting them from the sun with parasols, are walking downhill through a sloping orchard. They wear light-coloured dresses in an old-fashioned cut, nipped in at the waist, with leg-of-mutton sleeves. One of them waves a leafy branch about her hat and upper body to keep horseflies away. Crinkled hazelnut leaves give off a heady fragrance, made all the richer by the heat of the afternoon. The horseflies have long, greyish wings freckled with black. Walking ahead of the women is a little girl in a pale dress and wearing a boater made of wide, flattened stalks of gleaming straw woven in a chevron pattern. She is holding a bouquet of wild flowers...

I let myself get carried away with the reading. But when I look up I notice that Monsieur Dautrand's eyes are closed not because of the 'intensity' of his concentration, but because he's well and truly asleep. His hands are still behind his neck, but his elbows have sagged noticeably. A soft snoring sound coming from his mouth leaves no room for doubt. And it's not just the snoring: there are also a couple of iridescent bubbles, the sort you'd get from playing with soapy water, and a tiny thread of saliva. A busy and powerful man he may be, but he's now reduced to his most basic state, unmasked. And actually why not? I sympathize, in a way. His life must be really testing, overwhelming and exhausting. And perhaps joyless. Of course he needs to let go completely from time to time. And that's what this is, the 'mask' has fallen away. But without losing any of his good looks. Because I'm going to say it again: this is a good-looking man. I don't know what life may have thrown at him, but attractiveness won't have been a problem. It really must be his restlessness that's ruined everything, the excessive importance he gives himself. But, thank God, here, like this, asleep and with his saliva bubbles, everything falls away, comes undone. All that's left is his childish and slightly slumped handsomeness.

I give a little cough. He wakes up. Lifts his eyelids wearily. I think he'll show signs of embarrassment or awkwardness, make some comment about Claude Simon, but no, he leaps to his feet, almost jumps on me, makes me drop the book. Close it, he says, put it down, there, on the side. Let's forget about that. There's no question that it's admirable writing, perfectly admirable... but, how can you expect?... Can't you see that it's *you* that I want, not that book?... And I can indeed see. He's up against me, squeezing me, pressed to me, trying to take me in his arms, reaching for my lips. Meanwhile his mouth is spouting half-formed, half-jumbled words. Since you were last here, he's saying, I can't stop thinking about you... Do you hear me? I'm not just saying that, it's the absolute truth... I can't help it... It's not my fault, it's yours. You should just stop looking so deceptively innocent and so fantastically seductive... Do you understand?... Who could resist you?... Certainly not me... Look at you... He drags me rather brutally over to the large mirror at the end of the room and makes me look at myself. You're sensationally alluring – I hope you don't mind my saying so – and you should be aware that I've no intention of leaving it at that... Don't you think we go well together?... (He leans his head on my shoulder, there's something endearing about the ridiculous image in the mirror.) Look, we could make a handsome couple… Marry me, that would be the thing to do, because I'm free… I obviously have to give him an answer: But, alas, I'm not.

He looks devastated. He lets me go, runs his hand through his hair, mussing it up, moving his hand in a way that I can now see is a habit. You're not free, he says, that's terrible! Are you married? Yes, I am. I hadn't thought of that, he says. I never think of anything, I'm thoughtless, I must be mad. It's this life of mine that does it to me. I can't go on like this. The balance sheets and trading accounts, I'm in over my head! It's got to change. But you're not wearing a wedding ring? I don't wear one, but I am married. He adopts a devastated, miserable expression: If you're not free, could you still be a *little bit* free? I ask him what he means by that. Speedy reply: A few moments of your life for me… It would be so wonderful, so exceptional… to hold you in my arms… What a dream… how intoxicating… He's back on the attack now, pressing against me, squeezing me again. He seems very piqued, completely put out: Surely you're not just a *reader*, though?… I look him right in the eye and say: Yes, I am actually a *reader*. He releases his grip: OK, then, read.

He goes back to his armchair. I go back to *Lesson in Things*.

Self-seeded oats and grasses swished by their long skirts make an abrasive sound. This little group walking in single file across the hillside leaves behind it an irregular wake in whose depths the grass eases only slowly back upright…

He interrupts me and says, almost as an order: Read the first sentence again. Rather pleased, thinking he's starting to take an interest in what I'm reading, I do as I'm told:

Self-seeded oats and grasses swished by their long skirts make an abrasive sound…

Another interruption. And a change of tone. He gets up from his armchair again. You see, he says, a sentence like that just *kills* me! Those long skirts, with their abrasive sound, they're killing me! That's how bad things are for me! I've got a shiver running from my head down to my feet, a quiver of longing washing over me (he actually said that: 'a quiver of longing washing over me' – he's not such a stranger to literature as I might have thought)… Beautiful, isn't it?… But it's sad too, fantastically sad… That's how bad things are for me… Two little snippets of a sentence and I'm in pieces… It's just, dear Madame, believe it or not, I haven't made love for six months… (His expression's now so heartbreaking that I think he's really going to cry this time.) As I told you, I'm totally alone… in a complete emotional and sexual desert… He's come closer to me again, has made me put down the book, but has settled for taking my hand. He's kneeling at my feet on the carpet, holding my hand. He brushes his lips over the tips of my fingers: If you wanted to help me, to do something for me… I remember how you looked the other day… that skirt, your legs… You could save me, he says, please save me!… I'm beginning to feel open to compassion. I take off my glasses, lean forward and offer him my mouth.

That may well have been unwise. Once again I gave in to what Philippe calls my 'good nature'. I'll have to have a talk with him. I've already said he's an open-minded husband, and is far too busy with his aerological engineering to worry much about me; but I do still need to talk to him.

I talk to him. I choose my moment during a rather dull programme about volcanoes – a subject he adores – but this evening, despite the spectacular eruptions, despite the narrator Haroun Tazieff's rough-hewn eloquence, he's snoozing, having come home late after a busy day. I switch off the TV and ask him to listen to me. He grudgingly cooperates. I explain the situation. He very quickly gets the gist and gives the reaction I expected. This man, he says, you can *do* him (forgive me, but that's his word) if you want to, I think he's bound to be *delighted* (that's his word too), but I advise you to be very wary and really think it over first. Now, if you're happy to, let's get some sleep. I'm furious. No, I say, we're not going to get some sleep. I'm not tired and I want to talk! Philippe never wants to talk. He gazes wistfully at the television screen. He doesn't like seeing it all grey and empty. I suspect it gives him a genuinely painful panicky feeling. But he'll have to put up with it this evening. The problem I've just described to him warrants more than a few words and a couple of cobbled-together sentences. He doesn't seem to think so, and I can tell his eyelids are heavy. His eyelashes are fluttering. Wonderful eyelashes. He's absurdly attractive, but sadly makes absolutely no use of the fact. Which leaves me standing in front of him, between his chair and the TV, completely lost for words. Still, I do need to get out of this stalemate before he goes to sleep in front of me – he's yawning dangerously – so I go all out with: Right, so that's OK, I can go for it?

You do what you like, he says. But watch yourself, don't lose control and, more importantly, don't forget I love you. He's on his feet and already heading for the bedroom. But he changes his mind, probably because he has something to add. After a moment's hesitation he says: You know, you were starting to have a proper job, it really seemed to be taking shape and making you happy. Don't go and ruin it all for this boloney. *Boloney* is his word too. But what on earth can it mean here? Anyway, I can tell he's not going to add to that. He's already pulled his sweater off over his head and is going to bed.

It's a bit more complicated with Sora. Because I consult him too. You can't say I'm taking this lightly. I'm garnering opinions. My 'old master', as was to be expected, is dismayed. But I've long known that where I'm concerned and on this sort of subject, he doesn't think objectively. You're going to ruin everything! He's saying exactly the same as Philippe, but in a different way and not in the same voice. And definitely with very different concerns and ulterior motives. But, once over the initial shock, he affects complete detachment, perfect neutrality. You do what you want, however you want! Again, the same as Philippe. I ask you.

They're all the same. They all respect my freedom. I don't think I'll ever find a father again: since mine slipped away quietly I haven't had the least opportunity to replace him. Well, Marie-Constance, you be a big girl, be a grown-up, and decide for yourself how you behave! That's me talking now, I hope you get that – it's not Sora. He's sitting there quiet as a mouse. He's far too put out by what I've told him to say anything. But I push him. I need him to play his *part*. I need him to give me his opinion. Yes, Monsieur Sora, you have to. Go on, speak, say something.

Then all of a sudden, out of nowhere, he speaks. A scalding stream of Sartre-style logic in which I can make out: Dear girl, we're always free in life and we're always alone. Do what you like, do whatever tickles you, but in that case don't ask for advice... If it tickles you to sleep with this man, go ahead... It's clearly all he wants... I did warn you... It's your problem, not mine... It's just some tickles can cost you dear... can have all sorts of incalculable consequences. You know that as well as I do... so weigh it all up properly... From the moment you decided to run that ad, I told you anything could happen. It was bound to attract lunatics, maniacs, perverts... especially a managing director with too much time on his hands, whatever he may tell you, and probably going into liquidation or bankrupt... separated, divorced even, and the most unbelievable crybaby... If I've understood this right, if I've followed what you've said... maybe you're attracted to him, maybe he looks like a matinee idol. That's your business... Take your chances... You've only ever done what you wanted anyway, haven't you?... But if you really want an opinion, I'll give you one: look carefully at what you're getting into… and don't forget that you ran that ad to *read* to people – in other words, to have an interesting, respectable job… It was attempting the impossible but it was beginning to look as if it might succeed… at least, from what you said… so, in my opinion, you'd do better to stick to *reading*!

He's finally come out of his shell. He's said what he meant. Stirred himself. I'm really, truly happy. I look at him with a sort of impassioned admiration. His face is flushed with emotion. This is much better than with Philippe. *He*'s making a commitment. I think that, quite apart from the years binding us together, I still have very strong feelings for him. But why do I always want to do the opposite of what he says? I think I've made up my mind.

The first session with Clorinde goes very well. If I can venture to say that, because we'll have to see how it develops. When I arrive, the child is waiting for me alone at home and greets me like a grown-up. She explains that her mother won't be home until the evening, late, but everything's organized, that we can use this room, if I'm happy to sit in here, and then have some tea later. It is in fact her own little bedroom that she shows me into, and the view from the window confirms what I noticed on the way here: it's a beautiful day. A magnificent winter's day. Cold but luminously blue.

And it's this weather that plays a trick on me. Indeed, I've only just begun reading *Alice* before Clorinde starts to show peculiar signs of agitation. For example, I finish the following passage:

> *Alice had not a moment to think about stopping herself before she found herself falling down a very deep well.*
>
> *Either the well was very deep, or she fell very slowly, for she had plenty of time as she went down to look about her, and to wonder what was going to happen next. First, she tried to look down and make out what she was coming to, but it was too dark to see anything; then she looked at the sides of the well, and noticed that they were filled with cupboards and book-shelves; here and there she saw maps and pictures hung upon*

pegs. She took down a jar from one of the shelves as she passed; it was labelled 'ORANGE MARMALADE', but to her great disappointment it was empty...

And Clorinde jumps to her feet and rushes to the kitchen, I hear her rummaging about, moving things, probably a set of steps, opening a cupboard, and then she comes back triumphantly, holding a pot of marmalade. I tell her to put it away quickly and come back and listen to the story. She does as she's told, comes back, drops on to her little chair, where she sits with her arms crossed and seems to be listening, but when I embark on the bit about Dinah the cat chomping on bats, she leaps up again and from I have no idea where, the storeroom perhaps, produces a tiny bluish-coloured cat asleep in a basket. It's a cat! she cries, putting the basket right under my nose. She was born a week ago. I look at the kitten, say how sweet it is, even stroke it rather reluctantly, without waking it, then ask Clorinde to put it back where she found it. I start reading again. This is when we come to the passage about the golden key:

Suddenly she came upon a little three-legged table, all made of solid glass; there was nothing on it except a tiny golden key, and Alice's first thought was that it might belong to one of the doors of the hall; but, alas! either the locks were too large, or the key was too small, but at any rate it would not open any of them...

No point reading on! Hearing these words, Clorinde gets up for the third time and goes to the front door to fetch the key to the house. She brings it over, shows it to me, and this is when the ill-fated weather comes into play. What if we went out? she says. It's such a beautiful day! I never go out and Mummy won't be home till late… She looks so adorable all of a sudden, with her pink cheeks and her eyes like a mechanical doll's – I can't resist. I say yes. Unthinking. Irresponsible. Yet again. But it's true that it's a glorious day, the sky's really blue through that window, and it seems to be calling us, beckoning us insistently. There's the key, dangling from a key ring in Clorinde's hand, and – like some magic object – it makes the decision: we're going out. Apparently there's a giddying funfair at the park, with rides and games and stalls and stands. Clorinde is madly excited. As for me, I'm clearly plain mad. While I put on my fur-lined jacket and tie my scarf, the child goes off into her mother's bedroom and I can hear her opening drawers. I call her rather anxiously and she says she needs to fetch her scarf too, and a hat that her mother often lends her. She's taking her time, seems to be scurrying around a great deal, riffling through drawers, but eventually she comes back, pretty as a picture in her little coat, wearing the woollen hat which comes right down to her eyes and a scarf wound around her neck at least three times, and carrying a pair of gloves she's about to put on. She's ready. And I'm ready too. We look to see we haven't left anything untidy in the house, no light left on unnecessarily, no tap running. And we leave. We won't say anything to Mummy, Clorinde whispers, it's our secret! My only answer, as I close the door, is to ask her for the key because we absolutely mustn't lose it.

Now we're out in the chilly, sun-drenched street. We take a bus to get to the park more quickly. Clorinde seems enchanted by every little detail – passers-by, advertising posters on the bus, the bus driver, the shop windows all ready for Christmas, fir trees decked out with stars and tinsel. Then, all of a sudden, the fair! She wants a go on every ride. On a glossy horse, a chrome motorbike, a spacecraft bristling with antennae, a multicoloured rocket. I'm so worried she'll do something silly I end up getting in with her, so there we both are, two mad things together, to the astonishment of onlookers (well, in my case, at least), carried away, caught up in the excitement of it. I've already paid for a good many rides, so Clorinde, behaving like a proper little lady, says she'd like to pay for some too, that she's got lots of coins in the pockets of her coat; she made a point of taking them out of her money box before we left. We set off again, on a giant caterpillar this time, then on swings that lurch through the air. It doesn't seem to unsettle Clorinde's stomach, and she also wants to do justice to the stalls selling delicious treats, gorging on caramel and lollipops, daubing herself in candyfloss, sipping a Coca-Cola and crunching on sugared almonds. I'm starting to get seriously worried, but reassure myself with the thought that, in order to be running amok like this, the child must usually be deprived of these things that other children so enjoy. And that her developer-mother would do well to give her a bit more of her time and attention.

I couldn't have guessed that at the exact moment I have this thought, by an extraordinary twist of fate, this busy woman is coming home early, having had three of her afternoon meetings cancelled. And she's coming home all thrilled and enthusiastic at the thought of finding her little girl with her *reader*, because it's the day of their first session. So – horror of horrors – this is what's happening while we're spinning round on rides. She rings the bell. No one opens the door, no one answers. She lets herself in with her own key. Finds the house deserted. She goes into Clorinde's bedroom, sees the little chair turned to face the small bench seat, but empty of course and looking oddly abandoned, and the book of *Alice's Adventures in Wonderland* thrown to the floor, open. She goes into every room, opens every door. Nothing. No one. Not a sign. No message. Terror rises through her stomach, up to her throat, then to her head, instantly turning into all-out panic, surprising in a professional woman accustomed to keeping a cool head. But, there's no denying it, she's gripped with panic and has just one outlandish, appalling, haunting sentence ringing in her ears: My daughter's been abducted! A hypothesis confirmed, when she checks in the drawer and cupboard, by the absence of Clorinde's clothes: coat, scarf, hat and gloves. Not a shred of doubt: that dangerous woman dressed her up all warm and snugly the better to *abduct* her. To take her away, drag her off, steal her. That's what comes of letting yourself be lured in by some pathetic ad and, with the best intentions in the world, entrusting your child to a stranger. To the first-comer. A specialist in abductions and kidnappings. Perhaps one of those miserable lost souls obsessed with their monstrous fixations who, never having had any children of their own, steal other people's without a second thought.

Or a consummately experienced crook who's now preparing to ask for a vast ransom. Madame Property Developer is horrified, despairing, outraged, furious with herself for her inconceivable irresponsibility. She can feel tears surging to her eyes at the thought of what her little Clorinde might be suffering, wonders whether she should call the police, but, when she's about to reach for the telephone, goes back into her bedroom, on one final straight-thinking businesswoman's reflex, to see whether anything's been taken from the top drawer of her chest of drawers, where she keeps a few pieces of jewellery and precious things... and sees that her jewellery has indeed vanished.

At this point, in order to keep up with events, you have to picture Clorinde, cheeks ablaze, between two funfair rides, suddenly opening her coat, unwinding her scarf and beaming with delight as she reveals two strings of pearls around her neck, along with an emerald pendant and a gold ring set with a diamond, then taking from her pockets all sorts of glittery things, explaining that she didn't only bring a stock of coins but also rings, brooches, earrings, cameos, expensive gems, and these are all things, she says, her mother lends her from time to time and she felt like bringing with her today, because they were having a little party, and girls should always be as beautiful and dressed up as possible for parties. The *reader* is thunderstruck, rooted to the spot by the sight of her wearing all this jewellery, its twinkling lighting up her neck, her little chest, her ear (where she's just attached a golden earring) and her hands.

Meanwhile the mother has discovered that the drawer is, of course, empty. In a flash it all becomes clear. Not only abduction, but organized robbery. Well, that'll teach her! She picks up the telephone, calls the police and in a quivering, shaking, halting voice summarizes the whole situation. The officer can't interject a single word into her trembling stream of pain and anger. He asks her to keep her cool and to come to see him as soon as she can. He also asks for descriptions of Clorinde and me.

Luckily, less than an hour after this Clorinde is back and so am I. The explanation process is difficult, but it does take place. I plead guilty, but I also plead that I was intoxicated by the beautiful winter weather, it went to my head, and I was so happy to be with such a lively little girl, who was almost magically persuasive, and so kind and dazzlingly intelligent. I lay it on as thick as I can in an attempt to disarm the mother. But she won't be disarmed. She's beside herself, screaming, increasingly hysterical, calling me every name that comes into her head. I tell her her jewellery is here, not a single item missing, I offer to spread it out on the table so she can count every piece. A suggestion that makes her all the more furious, makes her shout even louder. She does, however, manage to interrupt her own vocal outbursts sufficiently to tell me that when she found the apartment empty and the drawers broken open (in her words), she was struck by such powerful emotions she nearly had a heart attack, which isn't just a men's problem as people so often believe, but something that can strike down active, responsible women like herself, not lazy useless idiots like me – I should know that, I should consider myself informed. She sits down, struggling to breathe and mopping her brow. If she dies it will be my fault. Her face has fallen apart, her perm has collapsed over her forehead, her splendid high-flying woman's composure has cracked. Clorinde, realizing the extent of her misdemeanour, starts crying too, then screaming and rolling on the ground. I can't think how to contain this disaster now.

Days go by. We're into the new year. I hope the Christmas celebrations were fun for Clorinde and that her mother has forgiven her everything. But I'm unlikely to see either of them again any time soon. Unless they call back. Unless they come looking for me. In the meantime, I mustn't lose the few 'regulars' I've managed to hook. In fact, I'm on my way to my managing director today. He's more hooked than anyone else, we've all grasped that, but by something other than reading. I've made my decision and I'm ready. But I must still try to bring him round to literature. If Claude Simon is a bit too much for him, I could try to reel him in with Perec. That's what I've decided to try. I've chosen a few pages of W. I've read the passage over and over. It's perfectly accessible and he should like it. I even recorded it in the echo chamber and, at this very moment, I'm walking along with a Walkman so I can listen to my text. It makes the busy street look wonderfully animated and I can cut out the noise of cars. The well-padded earphones also give my ears much-appreciated protection from the cold. It's still dry and bright.

I can tell straight away that dear Michel is not disposed to listen. But he really will have to go through with it. He's never heard of Perec, but I sing the author's praises. We sit ourselves down and, having assured him that with a book like this he'll be truly impressive at his dinners, I begin:

> *I have no childhood memories. Up until the age of about twelve, my story could be told in a couple of sentences: I lost my father when I was four, and my mother when I was six; I spent the war in various boarding houses in Villard-de-Lans. In 1945 my father's sister and her husband adopted me.*
>
> *For a long time I found this lack of a personal story reassuring: it had a dry objectivity, was transparently self-evident, but what was it protecting me from, if not the very story of my life, from my true story, my own story...*

He interrupts me abruptly and I can tell immediately that it will be difficult to get any further. My own story... my own story... he says, almost tripping over the words. I don't know what this man's talking about... but *my* story, my one, as I've already told you and I'll tell you again, is terrible, desperate... This woman I gave everything to, sacrificed everything for... and who left me... in a way I don't even want to, *can't* even describe... and now this emptiness... and this dreadful work life, this world of business meetings and meals and journeys which just make the emptiness even more cavernous... I can't go on... I don't want to listen to any more or hear any more... Come! I ask him where. To my bedroom, he replies. He's already by my side and, grabbing my arm, starts to tug it not altogether discreetly.

It's obvious that today he's planning to get on with it. To be quick and efficient.

As I've already made up my mind to agree to this, he doesn't have to fight too hard. So here we are in the bedroom and very soon in bed. I've undressed quickly, perhaps that was wrong, but at this time of year I like to slip between the sheets and blankets as quickly as possible. He's clearly taken aback and doesn't have the nerve to take off his clothes in the same way. He must be finding the silence unbearable, because he gives a couple of little coughs, then comes to sit on the edge of the bed and takes my hand. I'm so overcome, he says, so overcome... I would never have believed it! He's holding my hand as you would an invalid's, a feverish child's, as if taking my pulse, but it's perfectly clear that his pulse is the one racing. When I eventually speak, I simply say: Come.

He finally makes up his mind to get to his feet, not without a lot of hesitation, and heads for the bathroom. I can hear running water, a lot of water. Clothes falling. Then the sound of a bottle being moved, set down on the basin or the side of the bath, the patting sound of a hand presumably applying some alcohol or lavender water to stubbly cheeks or chubby flanks. He comes back with a large white towel secured around his waist. He goes over to the window, draws the curtain. He's still hesitating, not yet decided to come over and join me. And yet he does. He's barely in bed before I, in turn, slip to the bathroom, with his permission. He watches me walk across the room with something like astonishment, making his eyes grow wider and wider. I run some water too. And I too come back clad in a white towel that I've knotted firmly on my hip. I make a detour via the living room to fetch the book, two books even. Getting back into bed, I say: We're going to go back to a bit of Perec, and why not some Claude Simon too. I'm sitting between the sheets, leaning against a pillow, leafing through one of the books, with my glasses on my nose. He's lying beside me. For pity's sake, he says plaintively, don't be sadistic! Still, I read a few lines. Oh, your voice! he interrupts me. It's all down to your voice! It gets right into my bone marrow. I've never heard a voice like yours, Marie-Constance. It gives me shivers all over! You have no idea. He takes my hand and puts it authoritatively on to his chest: a handsome, well-thatched torso. When I draw back my hand he looks put out, disappointed. He jumps up, announcing that he's going to get his cigarettes. He doesn't seem embarrassed to be walking across the room naked. He's rather fine: well put together, solidly built. He comes back with his packet of Marlboros and puts it on the bedside table, along with a lighter and an ashtray. I've picked up the book again, so he sits down on the bed next to me, takes a cigarette and lights it, probably to demonstrate his irritation.

Then, all of a sudden, that's it! He stubs out his cigarette in the ashtray, snatches my book and my glasses from me, and throws himself on me with no warning. He clasps me, crushes me. What was bound to happen inevitably happens. Try as he might to hug me, squeeze me and kiss me all over, on the mouth, in the ear, on my neck, my breasts, all with terrifying, avid urgency, he achieves only lucklustre results. He realizes this, turns away abruptly and moves back to his side of the bed with a pathetic expression on his face. I knew it, he says, I could have guessed... and yet you're *so* beautiful, so gorgeous, so exceptional... It's precisely because I want you so badly... why I'm so manically impatient... so desperately impatient it's sick... You have to understand I'm in the same situation as someone who hasn't eaten for three months and is suddenly presented with a sumptuous display, a royal feast... He can't eat a thing... He's dying of hunger... but his stomach won't take it, his throat won't accept it... What sort of reply could I give except: Am I a sumptuous display? A royal feast?

Rather than pursuing this conversation, he's opted to sit up in bed and return to his cigarette. I warn him not to burn the sheets and I commit the spectacular blunder of telling him that his wife should have taught him not to smoke in bed. Not only does he look exasperated, but he gets up yet again, as if operated by a spring, goes over to a set of shelves facing the bed and turns a photograph of a woman – a rather spruce specimen, I think – towards the wall. I forgot! he says with something close to anger, she's got no business being here any more... specially today! Then he heads back to bed all miserable and sad and tragic with a: But do *I* have any business with anything any more? Do I have any business with life any more?

I say yes, of course he has, I try to comfort him, to persuade him to come back beside me. He does, but with despondency written all over his face. I don't know why I get the feeling this despondency could turn into violence at any moment. So I reassure him, telling him that what's happened to him is completely normal and not at all serious. He just needs to calm down, to relax, to let his body and mind unwind, and a bit of reading can't fail to be beneficial with that. I'm sitting, naked once more. I've picked up my glasses and Perec. He listens:

> *Once again the traps of writing were set. Once again I felt like a child playing hide-and-seek who does not know what he fears and wants more: staying hidden, being found…*

Shyly, but actually quite firmly, he puts a hand on one of my breasts. But rather remotely. With no verve or ardour, with no flourish of conquest. Because it's the procedure: *deliberately*. I surmise that he needs to feel both bold and calm. I abandon the book, take a deep breath and look all around the room through my clear lenses. A lovely room with a light-pink tint to the walls overlaid with striking black appliqué designs. Simple, geometric furniture. A lozenge-shaped mirror in which I can see myself, and can see his hand on me. A painting on the wall, reminiscent of a Mondrian. A beautiful touch-tone telephone in a gleaming mauve, within reach of the bed. An extremely elegant single-stem crystal vase next to the back-to-front photograph. I didn't take the time to notice all these things. I now identify them one by one. The room is large, comfortable, orderly. The cleaning lady must be diligent. It feels good, us being here in this bed. But we need to do something. He must be thinking that too, because the pressure from his hand is increasing noticeably. At the same time he tells me in a deep, husky, slightly strangulated voice that I have beautiful, very beautiful breasts.

I suggest that we throw off the covers because it's better to be on show than hidden when making love, not too wrapped up anyway. And this can help with better preliminaries. Even though he looks a bit surprised by this suggestion, possibly wondering whether it's disguising some trap, he says he agrees but that it might be a good idea to turn the heating up so that *I'm* not cold. He gets up right away and turns the control knob on the radiator. He even offers to plug in another heater if I'd like it. But I wouldn't like it, the room's already warm. If he really wants heat, I can offer him my body heat. He seems to grasp this because, once back by the bed, he throws himself on me again. But this is a reverse attempt. Perhaps to avoid the previous disappointment. What I mean is he launches his head at my stomach, kissing it and licking it, literally, with unusual violence, all around my navel (whose asymmetry he doesn't seem to have noticed – it hasn't put him off his stride anyway), then he lunges frantically, dizzyingly, towards my pussy, burying his head between my thighs as I spread them as wide as I can. A giddy feeling gradually seeps over me, reaching the small of my back, soon to rise higher still, pounding, breaking like a wave over my throat, the nape of my neck, my brain. There he is then, going down on me, taking me into his mouth with demented enthusiasm. But I forgot to say, when introducing myself earlier, that I have extraordinarily curly and densely packed pubic hair. Unfortunately, one of these hairs must have got in the wrong place on his tongue or even in his throat, because all of a sudden, at the very height of passion, he's afflicted with a terrible paroxysm of coughing, as if something's 'gone down the wrong way', and that is sadly what has most likely happened. He lifts his head, keeps on and on coughing, suffocating, unable to catch his breath and going so red that I start to panic. I really have to gather my wits and return to a more decent position. I ask whether there's anything I can do for him, suggest helping him to the bathroom. So here we are at the basin. I've just turned on the light and he's still coughing. I look inside his mouth and down his throat to see whether I can find the foreign body that's causing so much trouble. I need a torch, and probably some tweezers, some sort of tool, to extricate it. I do my best with my fingers, burrowing in deep, delving down, and I must achieve something because he suddenly seems to be relieved, stops coughing and can breathe properly again. I advise him to drink some water straight away. He fills his toothbrush glass from the tap and drinks. Things have obviously improved.

He doesn't look as if he really knows where he is. His eyes are red, his hair all awry. But the trauma of this incident seems to have released him from the fantasies, the obsessions of his imagination, and it is an entirely relaxed and docile man that I lead back to bed, holding him by the hand. He lets me take the lead, abandons himself, and that's a very good thing. I gently take possession of his body, stroking him from head to foot, while he lies, eyes closed, allowing a soft murmur of pleasure to filter through his lips and, after a few moments, I have no trouble crouching over him and straddling him as only a lover can.

I sit up to my full height so that I can see him, and I feel resplendent, regal, mistress of the situation. He's breathing more and more deeply, almost panting, and the murmur has turned into a sort of muted drone. I tell him that where lovemaking is concerned you mustn't rush anything, must make it last, and I suggest we go back to our interrupted reading, seeing as the book's right here, somewhere among the covers. I look for it, find it, open it and read (even though I have a lot of trouble controlling, *holding*, my voice):

> W *is no more like my Olympian fantasy than my Olympian fantasy is like my childhood. But, in the network woven up between them, as in my reading of them, I know that what has been written down and described is the path I have trodden, the development of my story and the story of my development…*

This clearly isn't a very propitious initiative. I can feel, deep inside me and most unequivocally, its negative effects. Besides, he's found the strength to open his eyes and give them an imploring glint as he says: No, no! Anything, but not *reading*, not now! I'm sure he's right. The book disappears. Everything else comes back. And goodness knows what sort of chasms and insanities are taking shape in him and me alike. I ask him to keep his eyes open, for as long as possible. He tells me it's very difficult, like trying to look at the sun. I insist all the same. I want him to see my face as I can see his. He looks at me. I can't tell whether his expression is tender or pained. I engage him in gentle conversation, trying to get him to understand that the merits of reading are not as dissimilar to those of lovemaking as he might think. He says that may be so, but right now he loves me and that's it. He knows he does, is sure of it. I try not to let my features melt, go beyond my control, or let my voice drown. I want to keep my eyesight and the power of speech. He's stopped talking now, has put his hands on my hips and is pressing with all the strength of the despair that he so wants to call love. I put my own hands on his shoulders and, with my face hovering above his, tell him calmly he shouldn't have any illusions about me, I came to read books to him, just as he requested, and that I'll probably only ever come back to do just that. OK, fine, he says in a now barely audible voice. I can feel the enormity of a great tree of emptiness, pleasure and delirium growing within me. A rocking motion steals over my whole body: my hips, which he's now clinging to as if to a buoy, my buttocks and thighs, the small of my back and everything inside. It's like a boat, a journey. He opens his lips once more to beg for the journey not to end. I just have time to tell him it will end, like all journeys, before throwing back my head, into the deep water.

Shock, horror. I've been summoned to the police station. I wonder what on earth can be behind this. Could it be to do with regularizing my 'profession'? Or has my interlude with Michel Dautrand already caused a few waves, a few smears? You have to be careful with small towns: public life quickly gets confused with private life.

It's actually to do with the Clorinde business. I should have thought of that. But a month later I've good reason to believe the subject is closed, given that nothing has happened. Which is what I explain to the man who's just introduced himself as Superintendent Beloy and who's wearing his fifty-odd years well: soft leather jacket, sporty appearance, a bit of a force of nature from what I can see. I tell him this story is based on pure fiction, on the feverish imagination of a rather hot-headed woman, whose concern was probably justified, and on the fantasies of a precocious child. Is he at least aware that everything was settled the same day, that all the jewels were returned safely? He's perfectly aware, he reassures me, making the point that no complaint of any sort was lodged and that he has sufficient experience to have swiftly put the whole thing in proportion. Nevertheless, he says with a nod of his head, there was a telephone call from this lady, who, at least in the heat of the moment, seemed very alarmed, even though she called back later to say there were no longer grounds to follow up her call and, well, you know what routine procedures are like, particularly within the police force, which is working with hopelessly insufficient funds and in outdated – not to say archaic – conditions. We immediately launched a quick investigation, not all that quick if truth be told, because it's only getting anywhere now, and we found that you'd run an advertisement in the papers. We're not criticizing you in any way, I must make that clear, but this sort of advertisement is always interesting, or to be precise, it's the role of the police to take an interest, particularly when incidents like this occur. It was perfectly harmless, granted, and inconsequential... but, well, that's why I asked you to come by... to ask whether you could shed some light...

He's finished at last. I thought he'd never extricate himself from the convolutions of his sentence. He's looking at me with that wily-fat-cat-ready-to-pounce look that policeman are so good at adopting when they want to look understanding as well as showing they can't be fooled. Rather fine features. Bushy greying eyebrows but with a softness in his expression. But, Superintendent, I say, what do you actually mean? What's happened to freedom? Is my profession subject to specific regulations? He doesn't look best pleased with my reaction. Madame, he says, I'd first like to point out that it isn't a profession, and that's precisely why it's not subject to regulations; secondly, there has never been so much freedom in France as there is now. Just compare it to other countries with which you may sympathize, who am I to say. I am just saying it, but I could have said anything, it's mere conjecture on my part, but surely you know that a feeling of insecurity in our society has increased considerably, and that our dear fellow citizens are alarmed, and rightly so…

I stand there looking at him, speechless, so he adds: I say 'alarmed' because this lady, as I reminded you just now, was extremely alarmed. You believe that was down to her imagination or her daughter's mischievous exuberance, fine, all well and good, but it was also partly because of your negligence, wasn't it, would you accept that?… So, all I'd like to suggest is that you behave more cautiously in future… when exercising your *profession*… that's all I wanted to say…

Silence. The room is bare, the walls dirty. A typewriter is clacking away behind me. I turn round to discover that it's not a skirted typist at the machine but a grim-faced policeman. He's typing one-fingered while sucking on a cigarette butt and trying to see what's going on with me. But nothing's going on. What sort of answer can I give Superintendent Beloy? He wants the last word? He's got it. His telephone rings opportunely, giving him a splendid exit. He picks up, listens to what the person has to say with a knitting of his (bushy) eyebrows, and replies with bored indifference. It seems to be to do with a stolen car, a typical case as they always are and bound to be mundane, but the superintendent does everything he can to pose in front of me, to come across as detached, at his ease. At one point he draws the handset away from his ear and holds it there, suspended, flipping it slightly from side to side, while some poor pernickety voice shouts itself hoarse giving explanations to which he's not listening. Meanwhile he eyes me steadily, at length, exaggeratedly. This is threatening to go on for some time. But he puts his hand over the mouthpiece, gets up, leans towards me and, gallantly, thanks me and says I'm free to go. Even adding that he's very glad to have made my acquaintance.

Still, it does have to be said that I now have a profession and it's beginning to take shape. Not masses of customers, of course, but if I don't lose those I have (yes, if I don't *lose* them!), it could work out. So let's nurture them, one by one.

This afternoon I'm going to see La Générale, having not been there for a few weeks because she was knocked sideways by a bout of flu, but is, apparently, impatient to see me again. That's what the maid told me over the telephone. Well, I mean: the housekeeper. A strange character, as you well know. When I get there, she reiterates that La Générale's been impatient and adds that she's been impatient herself, because I bring the pair of them a light and warmth she can't quite pin down. It must be something about me, my presence, but more particularly my voice. She'd so love to sit in on the reading sessions. She'd been enthralled, enraptured. These compliments are addressed to me without any coyness, far more openly than on previous occasions. She looks peculiarly constricted in a severe shirt and a pleated skirt held tightly at her waist by a military-style belt. Her hair is more raked back than usual. And real sparks are flashing in her eyes. She turns abruptly to check her watch and tells me her mistress was all the more impatient because I'm late. I explain that the streets are very busy, there are all sorts of traffic jams, and I've had to leave my car quite far away and come on foot.

At this precise moment, La Générale opens her door, emerges from her bedroom looking distraught, grandiose and formidable, and, brandishing a newspaper, harangues me for not reading the papers, and to think I put ads in them myself! You would have known, Nouchka, she says, that there's an important demonstration by employees of the local bus company in our town today. It's organized by their union, and workers from the Thoms factory, which, as you know, is just down the road from here, and where they actually make buses, are likely to join them this afternoon… All I can hope is that they'll pass under my windows… In the meantime, if you don't mind, we're going to go back to our reading where we left off… I haven't lost the thread, despite this bout of flu, which had me absolutely floored (a proper Magyar thunder roll!)… I tell her that surely no sort of flu, not even a bad bout, could get the better of a constitution as strong as hers, and express my admiration for her vitality as well as her unfailing vigilance in political and trade-union issues. The creature, yet again, has melted away: and there I was thinking she was dying to listen to the reading.

Truth be told, it would have afforded her only very moderate pleasure, because I've had to return once more to a text by Marx which I started during the last session and which, in my view at least, is no more entertaining than the previous ones, even though it deals with desert island derring-do. It's a passage from *Contribution to the Critique of Political Economy*, in which he talks about Robinson Crusoe and bourgeois society. I read while the countess leans back against her pillows, drinking her tea:

The isolated individual huntsmen and fishermen, with whom Smith and Ricardo begin, are part of the eighteenth century's bland fictional writings. Desert-island stories or Robinsonades do not in any way, as some civilization historians like to think, express a straightforward reaction to excessive refinement and a return to a misunderstood natural state. No more than Rousseau's Social Contract *relates to a similar naturalism as it establishes inter-relationships and connections, in the form of a pact, between subjects that are naturally independent of each other. This is the outward – and the purely aesthetic – appearance of major and minor Robinsonades. They are rather an anticipation of 'bourgeois society', which had been developing since the sixteenth century and was taking giant strides towards maturity in the eighteenth century. In a society such as this, where free competition reigns supreme, the individual appears to have broken away from links to nature, while...*

I look up, surprised by a fairly tumultuous noise billowing up from the street and filling the room. The countess was right. She literally leaps out of bed, thrilled to think there may be demonstrators gathering right beneath her windows. Robinsonades, she exclaims with a sort of malicious glee, far too many Robinsonades! Even though you don't read the papers, you must have heard about the ecologists and these so-called greens... In Hungary they're called the blues... They're the modern Robinsons... They need to be confronted with the solid realities of the people, the street... Before I've had time to say anything, she heads over to the window, in her nightdress, draws the curtains and opens the shutters wide with such determination that I feel she's bound to commit some act of genuine madness or, at the very least, given the time of year, expose herself to a brutal drop in temperature which, at her age, could be fatal. What to do to restrain her? Her vehemence seems stronger than anything else. I briefly consider calling the servant but imagine this would probably be more trouble than help. All the same, I try to get the old lady away from the window. She takes the wind out of my sails with a: Leave me alone, I have it all planned!

She has in fact put several of the red flags from her collection under her bed. She moves aside the mauve cat, who's sleeping on one of them, and takes them out individually. And now she stands brandishing them at the window, apparently in a heightened state of excitement. She's leaning out so far I'm afraid she'll fall, and I clutch her nightdress to hold her back.

The demonstrators are indeed filing past in the street. They are carrying all sorts of banners, mostly for the transport union. Men and women walk arm in arm chanting slogans, some are wearing their work clothes, conductor's uniforms. I'm worried they'll take La Générale's untimely initiative as a provocation, and the march does in fact stop briefly under her windows, demonstrators gathering on the pavement, marking time with their tramping feet in a disconcerting way, looking up inquisitively towards the façade of the building. They're coming from every direction, forming a growing crowd. The countess looks thoroughly pleased and sweeps her ageing arms energetically from left to right, waving her historic flags, literally shaking the dust off them into the four winds. I don't know what to do. The crowd seems to be muttering angrily. But all of a sudden, no, it produces a huge sort of cheer, a swelling roar of approval. No one can ever have seen so many people under these windows. Nor heard such a clamour. La Générale turns to me with a radiant, imperious expression on her face, and asks me to fetch something else from under her bed, a cassette on which, she says, she has recorded the Internationale.

With the passing months my little business is beginning to acquire a degree of notoriety. Word of mouth must be operating. The fact is I'm quite frequently 'approached', even if I don't always respond. And that's a very good thing: I can choose. Besides, for now I'm happier keeping my regulars. But I can't help noticing the emergence of a different sort of request being addressed to me: community groups, retirement homes, arts centres and even hospitals have contacted me. I'm not just a 'person', I am becoming someone.

That may be what's eating Superintendent Beloy. He's gone and summoned me again. Still the same look. Still the same eyebrows. Still the same wily casualness. I wonder if he'll ask me to take out a patent this time. Or delve deep into my private life. But no. He wants to discuss that street demonstration outside La Générale's house. It wasn't long before word reached him. He has good informers. Very good sources of information. He feigns real dismay. What were you thinking, he says, that mad old woman stirring up the whole neighbourhood, waving red flags from her window and playing the Internationale… You were right next to her… don't deny it… You were seen… you were even photographed… First, I retort, La Générale is not a mad old woman and, second, she can do whatever she pleases, and that has nothing to do with my work. He nods, making it clear he's far from convinced. That's debatable! he says, perhaps implying that he knows more about this than he'll let on. I suggest he should make himself clearer.

He gets up from his desk, comes over to me, takes hold of an old rush-seat chair and sits down on it, putting his knees almost against mine so that we are facing each other in a way that he presumably hopes feels confidential and intimate. Don't you understand... Générale Dumesnil isn't just anybody... Her husband was a major figure, an officer, a man of prestige... He left a lasting impression on our town, having chosen to retire here and to support several local charities... We can't let all that be tarnished by the eccentricities of his widow, who, as you know, was the Countess Pázmány by birth, and who, by her own family's admission, has completely lost her mind... and may be swayed by dubious international influences... may have been manipulated... Respect her right to a peaceful old age, by all means! Don't shut her up in an institution, so be it! Let her have you reading to her in her own home, fine! But let her create a scene on the public highway, no! At this point, the superintendent has rather changed tone, becoming noticeably more forthright and aggressive. Oh, I say, so the countess created a scene on the public highway, did she? That's odd... because she wasn't actually the one demonstrating. He moves his chair closer until he really is touching my knees. Madame, he says, the Rives-Vertes neighbourhood is a nice area full of nice people, a 'bourgeois' neighbourhood, if that's a word you would use. Générale Dumesnil has lived there a long time and is even one of its not insignificant jewels... Just because an aberration on the part of our town planners agreed to a factory being built nearby, that's not enough for the unions to tramp in as if they owned the place and indulge in their farcical performances... Because it *was* just a performance, and the old fruitcake only whipped it up with her high jinks. These high jinks are typical of her and an embarrassment to her family and her neighbours... Forgive me, but that's called a *breach of the peace* and you were party to that breach... I don't get involved in politics, I'll have you know, my dear, but I do do my job as a superintendent!

I reply sweetly that I'm not his 'dear' and, less sweetly, that I don't know what he's talking about when he accuses me of causing a breach of the peace. He gets to his feet and peers down at me. I don't like people who quibble, and you quibble too much... You know perfectly well what I mean and what I'm talking about... Reading. Reading!... Reading's all very well, but that's not an alibi for whatever takes your fancy... It may be a way of making a living, but we've seen exactly where it can end up with this whole demonstration business. Granted, it was a ridiculous business, even more outlandish than the business with the little girl and the jewellery... I'm not going to make a meal of this... I'm not going to blow these incidents out of proportion... But this does make two incidents in a very short space of time... So here it is: I'd like to ask you yet again to be careful, sensible... That's all... You're a big enough girl to understand that!

I get up from my chair, stand over him and look down on him to demonstrate that I am indeed *big* enough. He sees me to the door of his cruddy police station and says goodbye with the assurance that, in any event and whatever he may have said, he finds me *very* likeable.

I haven't seen Roland Sora for a while. He's been on an assignment in Brazil. He was taking part in conferences, something he does very well all over the world, running seminars and joining round-tables. On his return he is more than expansive about the country. The sambas, the candomblé, the intermingling of African, American and Latin influences, the unisex styling, there's no stopping him. The wonderfully 'natural' quality Brazilian women have, so much stronger than what Stendhal claimed to find in Italian women. And the acute interest, everywhere you look, in the latest advances from this old Europe. This old Europe, it has to be said, is just the term! Since he's been back, everything here feels cramped and devoid of energy. Devoid of youthfulness. In spite of Brazil's economic rut and its struggles to achieve democracy, a feral sort of youthfulness reigns and a giddy excitement about the future. Although great swathes of poverty are widespread, there's hope and joy. And the magnificent tropical summer. We've hardly got to the end of winter here.

All of which means Monsieur Sora is as willing to hear the tale of my recent adventures as someone on Sirius is to take on board the latest anecdotes from Earth. I feel really uncomfortable sitting facing him in this office where he's been good enough to grant me a few minutes, despite the number of students thronging around his door since his return. I keep my mouth shut. Luckily, he kindly asks me *where I've got to.* Where have I got to? That's precisely the mystery. I tell him that with Dautrand the step has been taken. He's signing papers as I talk, pretending not to listen, then waggles his head slightly, as if to say that, given the inevitability of the situation, he can but bow to it or that, because he's still in Brazil in heart and mind and body, this sort of news has about as much impact on him as a dead leaf skimming along the ground. Is he drawing away from me? Has he had enough or even more than enough of my little incidents and confidences? That's the impression I suddenly have, as I sit facing his desk. I feel like getting up and leaving. Or crying, which would be worse.

But I keep talking. I tell him about my misadventure with Clorinde. And La Générale's unruly behaviour. With that, Sora stops his signing and lends me an appreciably more attentive ear. He looks amused. Perhaps deep down he's beginning to think, like the superintendent, that I'm on a slippery slope and I'm starting to be *a breach of the peace* in our delightful little town. Still, he should have the advantage over Monsieur Beloy of understanding that this is all down to the unpredictable workings of my job – surely to blame! – which consists of reading out loud things that are intended for silence. Where could that possibly end up? And if *he* doesn't know, who on earth would? It's true, now I come to think of it, that he'd rather see his books in their bookcases in his library than free to roam. He's spent so long taming them!

Either way, he's indulgent with me. Probably short of time but not daring to throw me out, he gets up, comes over to me and gives me a brotherly kiss on each cheek.

With Eric there's a routine now. Except, it has to be said, on his birthday, when his mother absolutely insisted I take part in a little private party, as if I were family. She even made a point of telling me there would be a 'surprise'. I came in a pretty dress, a silk dress, hoping Eric would like it and it would satisfy what I think is his taste in fabrics. And as a present I brought an anthology of contemporary French poetry which opens, as it happens, with a Francis Ponge poem called 'Dressing Things Up': it may be aiming a bit high for a boy his age, but ever since our conversation about Baudelaire he's kept on amazing me or, to be more precise, delighting me with his alert, emerging sensitivity to poetry.

A cake bristling with fifteen candles stands in the middle of the table along with a bottle of sparkling wine, some orange juice and chocolates, on a freshly ironed scallop-edged tablecloth. Eric's hair is tidier than usual, with a distinct parting. His mother isn't wearing an apron today, but the curlers in her hair have done their duty exceptionally well. I very quickly grasp that the father won't be joining the party, that he's been held up at work; so I won't be meeting him this time either. Some friends are coming, though. Perhaps that's the surprise. A sad surprise. They ring the bell, they come up the stairs, the door opens: a woman comes in accompanying a blind child. I'm introduced to him: I didn't want to tell you beforehand... This is Joël... he's a friend of Eric's. They were at the same clinic for a while, for very different sorts of therapy, as you can imagine, but they've stayed friends, very close friends. They've carried on seeing each other (she clearly realizes her mistake straight away, the incongruity of saying *seeing each other*, a flush of red colours her cheeks) and Eric, who must have mentioned him to you, wanted him to join us today, with his mother, here.

The situation strikes me as odd, but I say how pleased I am to meet them, and shake their proffered hands. I sit at the table in this peculiar gathering comprising the two mothers and their two incapacitated children. I suddenly feel excluded from proceedings, alien, and I wonder yet again what I'm doing here. But the cake is a triumph and everyone looks happy. In Eric's case, it's hard to be completely sure. In Joël's, how would you know? His face is infinitely gentle, and yet so inexpressive in its gentleness that it's difficult to imagine any emotion being written on it. He seems to me genuinely impossible to reach. His mother, on the other hand, is far from inexpressive. She's as pushy as the other one, but not in the same way. With a lot more composure and authority. And the moment she starts talking I get it. You're very well known among the blind, she tells me. You may not have realized it... but that's the way it is... It's probably because Eric has spoken so highly of you to Joël... he admires you so much... and Joël has told his friends about you... They'd really like you to come to the institute to read to them... They've already asked the director... There's nothing more valuable than reading to the young visually impaired, you must know that… There's nothing more valuable, particularly because a reader… if she has your qualities and talents… Wouldn't you say, Eric? Don't you think, Joël?… They have their own books, of course… they have their Braille alphabet… and nowadays they have records and tapes… but what could ever replace the warmth of a living voice like yours?… You really ought to be an angel and accept this offer… They're expecting you!

She's almost begging now. I don't know what to say. Joël is still lost in his blank gentleness. Eric's looking away. No one says anything. I have the peculiar feeling that there really is an angel among us in person. Perhaps it's one of the children – but which one? It's hovering, it's between us, above us, an insubstantial presence and yet it's an astonishing physical reality, a ruffling feeling, a sound of wings, impalpable and silky, in my ear, against my neck, on my skin, and a thin beam of light shining, quivering among us. Perhaps it's just the candles on the cake that Eric's mother has just lit. They're left to burn for a moment, then he has to blow them out, respecting the traditional ritual. Nothing's spared. His wheelchair is pushed right up to the table and Eric has to lean forward, with some difficulty it seems to me, to extinguish the little flames. Joël smiles slightly, his face turned towards the flickering glow as if he can make it out through his veiled pupils. Glasses are clinked together, big slices of cake passed round on plates, compliments exchanged, and best wishes, there's a pretence of laughter. I now feel exactly as if I'm in a painting done by goodness knows what sort of Bruegel, except that in the objects I can see and feel around me there's none of the rich texture of paint, or its colour, its warmth, its brilliance. No, I'm just in a peculiar place in an oddly constructed composition, I'm wandering around the picture like the foreign guest or the generous patron who's been deliberately shoehorned into a family scene. But there's nothing beautiful, except perhaps for Joël's absent eyes and Eric's sickly body. The picture is just of a pitiful little interior, with tatty furniture, things made of plastic or Formica, junk-shop glasses and plates, and glimpses of oilcloth through the openwork of the table-cloth. If it could at least turn itself into a Chagall, if I could fly, swim through space, be airborne, find myself hovering head-down under the ceiling!

The little birthday party reaches a sort of climax when Eric's mother tells me, without asking how I feel about it at all, that I'm now going to move through into the next room and read to the two boys, who can't wait, she claims, for this wonderful treat. She's got it all planned, all decided. The other mother nods in agreement with an inane smile and a no less emphatic air of determination. Besides, the two women seem to want to stay alone to chat. They want to relegate me to my job while at the same time entrusting me to a duty that they themselves could never fulfil, even though, through their children, it has acquired a remarkable aura of prestige.

So here I am in Eric's bedroom with the two boys. Well, I won't be making any concessions! I came with this book that opens with 'A Dress for Everything', so 'A Dress for Everything' it shall be. Mind you, I think or perhaps

someone implied that Joël is younger than Eric and probably not so mature in matters of the arts. And what of
Eric himself, lit up as his heart and mind may be by his
fifteen birthday candles, is he ready for such subtleties?
Either way, he's proud of this inaugural reading from a
book I've just given him. I begin:

> *If objects ever lose their appeal for you, then you
> should take a stance and watch the insidious altera-
> tions effected on their surfaces by the sensational events
> of light and wind which depend on the scudding of
> the clouds, and on whether this or that collection of
> daytime light bulbs goes out or comes on, the con-
> stant shimmering of layers, the vibrations, smokiness,
> exhalations...*

I look up. I've lost track of where I am. I've lost track of
where these light bulbs are, or the layers, the sensational
events of light. Back there, behind that door, on the table
where the candle flames guttered in the fragile exhalation
of a very young man, in all that counterfeit jollity? Or
somewhere else, outside, out in a sun and a wind unfamiliar
and inaccessible to either of these teenagers? Should I go
on? Eric says I should with a nod of his head.

> *And so learn simply to contemplate the daylight – above
> the earth and its objects, that is – those thousands of
> light bulbs or phials hanging from a firmament, but at
> every height and in every position, so that, instead of
> showing it, they hide it...*

I'm not sure I should go any further. I'd really like to have a reaction, a sign of approval perhaps. Eric's eyes are pinned on me. Is it beautiful? I ask simply, anxiously. And then he gives me an answer: Yes, it's very beautiful, but *he* can't know that because he can't see you.

Passion. It was predictable. Michel Dautrand has convinced himself he's crazy about me and is adamant he wants to take me with him to Zimbabwe, where he's been given an opportunity to put his company back on its feet thanks to exceptional circumstances. New mines have been dug there. He's going anyway. If it's to be with me, then he'll be happy, his life can come together again. If it's without me, it would mean being buried in oblivion in the depths of Africa: he'll go down to the bottom of those mines and never come back out, drowning himself in his work as others might in drink.

That's what he says as he sips his pure malt whisky. I'm next to him on the divan, half naked. He strokes my shoulder and every now and then tries to get me to take a few drops of the precious spirit: I only have to sniff it; I prefer the smell to the taste. I haven't kept the promises I made myself, I realize that. I've recapitulated, rebedded. But it's less out of weakness than consideration of this departure for Africa. I believe he truly will put the plan into action. He doesn't really have a choice, I think. Sooner or later, then, he'll disappear from my sight. His passion will fade, as all passions do. So I can carry on for a while with this agreeable little connection between us. We're both, it seems to me, benefiting from it. Besides, he has a cooler head than he wants to let on. He knows full well I won't be going to Africa. At the moment, though, he's doing everything he can to persuade me. His business will go well. The money will come pouring in. I'd have a lavish residence. As many houseboys as I wanted. The discreet charms of colonial life would be recreated for me, within the fairer modern framework of cooperation and free enterprise. I'd be loved, bejewelled, spoilt, feted. I'd be happy. Much happier than in a misfit's job in a loser's town with a husband who couldn't give a damn about me.

Here I strike back energetically. I sing Philippe's praises. I say that I've never entertained the tiniest thought of leaving him, that, in my opinion, Philippe's worth a thousand managing directors like him. I ask him to take that as read. He doesn't seem to understand, looks completely distraught. I think sometimes he hates me.

I need to make the most of moments like this to get back to our reading. My relationship with him has done nothing to sideline my educative concerns. Quite the opposite. It is a form of education. If he wants to make love with me, he first has to agree to *read*. Not necessarily to listen to me. To read himself, from his mouth, with his voice, if that suits him better. What matters is for him to fine-tune this knowledge which he himself claimed he so needed for his social life. Then I will have fulfilled my remit and been paid for my lovemaking troubles. Which, as luck would have it, are lovemaking pleasures. He seems to understand this, to comply with it. Each time he wants me to perform a particular favour, reading has to have its moment beforehand. For example, he sometimes indulges an aberrant desire to kiss my buttocks with cannibalistic frenzy. I insist that first he uses them as a lectern for a book from which he must read out loud for at least a few minutes. I'm currently lying on my stomach, naked, on the carpet in the large living room, close to the fire crackling in the fireplace. The book is where I've just said and Michel is lying on my thighs with his arms crossed, his chin up and his neck raised, and is reading diligently. The text I've chosen, because I feel sure we can't spend all our time on the moderns and that a managing director's education should embrace the ancients and the meditations of humanists on fate and chance, is a letter from Pietro Aretino to Pope Clement VII:

Most Holy Father, chance may well govern human destinies in such a way that, however provident he may be, no man has any power against it, but yet it loses its authority whenever God wishes to intervene. Whomsoever falls from as high as Your Holiness should turn to Jesus with prayers, and not against destiny with complaints. It was necessary that the vicar of Christ should pay with suffering and misery for the debt of other people's errors; and the justice with which Heaven chastises sin would not have been made clear to all people, had your imprisonment not borne witness of it. Take consolation, therefore, from your afflictions, accepting that it is by God's wish that you are at Caesar's mercy and that you can suffer both divine mercy and human clemency. For a prince who is ever strong, ever prudent, ever prepared for the insults of fate, one who has done all he can to parry its blows, it may be an honour calmly to bear all the misfortunes that adver-sity asks him to bear: then what glory shall be yours if, girded with patience and having surpassed this prince in wit, constancy and wisdom, you suffer what God's will imposes upon you...

The weather's very warm. I've come out into the countryside for a walk in the woods. There's nothing more astonishing than this turning point in the year when the first buds are still curled up in their resinous sheaths, just letting their green tips peep out. It's as if the whole world is suspended in a fragile balance and there's no telling which way it might swing. Landscapes are still hazy, misty. Luckily, smells are ahead of colours. There's already a fresh new smell rising up from the earth.

I've put on a pair of espadrilles, as if to encourage the spring, but with thick socks. I've left my car at the entrance to a small clearing and I'm walking over a carpet of fallen leaves. I can feel the clarity of the air in my lungs. Just my bad luck, a jogging enthusiast in a tracksuit pops out from behind a tree and in a flash the solitude that was all my own is snatched away. I watch him run off along the path, shoulders high, back arched, regulating his breathing. At least I'm lucky it wasn't Sora; we'd have had to have a conversation. If he'd felt like talking, and I can't be at all sure he would. I get the feeling I irritate him, that he's sort of sulking, or that Brazil really did turn his head – what I mean is turn his eyes away from me – and that he far from approves of my activities. Tough luck for me. I'd have done better to have gone back to university, started attending his seminars again, recycled myself. That's most likely what he would have wanted. And to make love with him, before he gets too old. Rather than with that illiterate specimen I'm wasting my breath introducing to literature. I miss every opportunity. Always get it wrong. It takes a Philippe to have the patience to put up with that. The sort of patience that only comes with aerological engineering.

The jogger is followed, at a respectable distance, by a woman I hadn't anticipated. His wife perhaps. She passes me, face red and held high, without seeing me. She's opted for shorts. Rather an attractive figure. Large breasts that don't slosh about too much as she runs. Long thighs supporting buttocks that make me envious. I'm reminded of Françoise and her gymnastics. She claims she manages to sit still at her typewriter only if she allows herself regular relaxation sessions for her forearms and shoulders. And sport, fresh air and the natural world are essential for that. She regularly goes running with her lawyers: sometimes one, sometimes the other, occasionally both. She's full of dazzling illusions about me. Even wearing Lucky's halter, I shone like a bright light in her eyes. She was convinced I'd go places with drama. I'd go places with my voice.

Well, here's the proof that I've gone places. I've gone as far as the middle of this small wood, and I really don't want to see another human being. After the husband, the wife... I hope there won't be a string of child joggers. All I want to see are trees. There's nothing quite like trees. I'd like to clean their trunks meticulously of their old bark, then hug them and kiss them, press my lips to their naked wood. Chew their young leaves the moment they appear. Scratch my face on dense thickets of evergreens. Walk on this earth without espadrilles or socks. Set off in search of grouse and stag beetles. Go deeper into the woods. Further still. And meanwhile allow my lips to utter these snatches, fragments, shards of things I've read that are dancing inside my head, these bits of pages I really ought to buckle down and learn by heart, if I want to give this profession of mine a bit more gloss, revenue and diversity. Oh, my God, who am I?

I thought nothing else could happen to me. That wasn't allowing for the calendar. La Générale had a surprise in store for me on 1 May. I arrive at her house as usual, having unsuspectingly accepted her suggestion that I should come and read to her on this date, and in the morning too: she told me the day had real significance for her and that she'd like to spend it with me.

I've hardly crossed the threshold before I sense tension in the air. Gertrude (I've spent six months not knowing her name) comes up to me with a riding whip in her hand and a distraught expression on her face, rolling her eyes so I can see virtually nothing but the whites. She hands the crop to me: Whip me! Seeing my astonishment, she says it again, lips aquiver: Whip me! She looks pale, and the way her hair is scraped fiercely back into a bun exaggerates the distress on her face. Now she's quivering all over. I soothe her, suggest she puts the whip back where it came from (on the shelves in the living room, it's part of the museum, a memento of the Général) and ask her for an explanation. She says she's ashamed of herself, that she's guilty of an abomination and deserves no better than the knout, that for a second time she's failed to anticipate one of her mistress's pranks and has led me, such a devoted reader, into a terrible trap. I think I can see that the 'first time' was the business with the union demonstration which scandalized the neighbourhood. What does the second have in store? Gertrude won't say. She falls to her knees before me, begs me to punish her, whip her. Besides, she adds, for me this fair punishment would be a pleasure. She starts tugging the bottom of her starched blouse from the waistband of her skirt, to bare her torso. I urge her to stop this ridiculous behaviour and tell me what's going on. She eventually makes up her mind to talk. Here it is: the countess has absolutely no intention of devoting herself to a reading session, she wants to go to the Labour Day demonstrations and is counting on me to go with her. She's already dressed.

Not believing my ears, I rush to the bedroom, open the door and what do I see? An ageing aristocrat from a bygone age looking at herself in the wardrobe mirror, trussed up in a tight black lamé dress that gives her spare tyres without denying her a degree of elegance, with a sort of boa tossed around her neck and a feathered hat on her head. She spies me in the mirror, turns round, comes over to me and says: Nouchka, you're going to take me to the Labour Day parade! It's so clear, so definitive, so peremptory that I can't see how to get out of it. Particularly as the countess has just added, with a wateriness about the eyes, that it may be her last Labour Day. I help her put on her old fur coat and hand her her walking stick. I try to put it off a little longer by saying I don't even know where we have to go, I've no idea where they hold this gathering. She grabs her handbag, takes out a piece of paper, a map with a line traced across it: the itinerary for the march. She's thought of everything. Anyway, she says, the procession is gathering outside the Mairie. If you don't have your car,

Nouchka, we'll take the bus. She drags me out. I think I can hear cries and lamentations and the stamping of feet from the kitchen.

It's a very long time since I saw a Labour Day demonstration. I have to admit that this one strikes me as rather pathetic. There's no crowd in front of the Mairie to listen to the breathless haranguing of a union representative who'd dearly love to motivate people heart and soul, but doesn't have the oratory means. La Générale's presence is therefore all the more noticeable. Not that she's trying to hide, mind you. She's incredible, robustly throwing her weight about, waving her stick, hailing a group of immigrant workers, probably road sweepers, and calling them 'comrades', wanting to buy some lily of the valley from a vendor, snapping up twenty stems in one go and handing them out around her, paying with a big banknote without expecting any change and fidgeting impatiently. People are whispering, muttering, pointing her out to each other. I don't feel very comfortable. But my discomfort is at its most acute when, once the customary rallying cheers are over and the procession is forming, she obviously intends to feature in its front line, on my arm, despite the embarrassment of the organizers, who don't seem to know how to handle this initiative of hers. Some discreetly ask me for explanations, which I'm quite incapable of providing. The procession eventually sets off and there she is in the first row, linked to me with one elbow and the secretary of the local trade union council with the other, limping slightly, and even having a little trouble putting one foot in front of the other, but radiant and clearly determined to see this through to the very end, albeit at the expense of inevitably slowing the pace of all the other demonstrators through the streets of our town. I twist my neck to check on her for fear she might faint in this throng of people. I can see that she's managed to pin some lily of the valley to one side of her coat, and to the other the red carnation and ear of corn that symbolize the Hungarian Uprising. People watching us march past are initially stunned to silence, but then applaud thunderously. Many of them seem to recognize her. They're even cheering from the windows to acknowledge her favour.

It feels as if this will go on for ever. But when we come to the Place de la Libération, just as we file around the flowerbed in the middle of the square, why do I have to go and see a little girl on the pavement waving her hat and scarf at me? It's Clorinde. For a moment I think I'm dreaming, caught up in some sort of hallucination where everything's jumbled up and flung together like in a kaleidoscope. But no, it really is her. It's so really her that she breaks away, starts running towards us, crosses the square and comes to join the procession. Now look how I've been framed, right and left, in the town centre, in this crowd, bang in the middle of the day, just in case I wanted to preserve my professional anonymity! I quake at the thought that, on top of everything else, Clorinde may have run away without a second thought again. Thank goodness, though, she reassures me under her breath. She tells me her mother's with her, and it was her mother who recognized me from a distance and suggested Clorinde should run over to me, and they both want our reading sessions to start again, they're waiting for me, I must come back. As I lean in to hear her better, she plants a hot fresh little kiss on my cheek. She smells of lily of the valley.

Another summons, a far from affable one, from Super-intendent Beloy. This time he's out and out angry. There's a policeman standing in his office and Beloy doesn't even ask him to leave when I arrive; the man eyes me with an ironic, wolfish glint. The superintendent wants to remain polite with me, courteous, he says, but he feels I've overstepped the permitted limits. That exhibitionism on Labour Day was barely credible. It affected the whole town, yes, *the whole town*. And I certainly can't go saying it was nothing to do with me. I was in the front row of the procession, supporting La Générale with my arm, none of that hap-pened by chance, impromptu. What have I to say in my defence?

He looks really furious. This must be serious. I wonder whether the policeman's going to put me in handcuffs. I reply, of course, that Labour Day processions are traditional and peaceful, and, as far as I know, it's not against the law to participate in them. He leaps (rather deftly, it has to be said) from his chair, sits on the corner of his desk and stares at me, pity tussling with the anger in his eyes. That's not what this is about, he says. Don't play all innocent, and don't play the fool either. Everyone has a right to join in the procession… What I want to know is why you drag this respectable woman… unhinged but respectable… into such incongruous situations?… Are you trying to be provocative? Is this a delayed contribution to the riots of '68?... Openly and publicly defying our town... because that's the overall impression, dear Madame... I've been sent letters, would you believe... I've got a drawer full... I've been collared by the family, who don't know what to do next... The local authorities aren't at all impressed... The regional authorities have been in touch, the national ones too... By now the Minister for the Interior will have been informed... things happen quickly by telephone, you know... and I'm actually the one who's responsible for public order and security here...

I ask him calmly whether the town's security was put in danger. The question infuriates him. Oh, oh, he says, you think you're very clever... but there are terrorists everywhere... usually hiding behind outward appearances that are above all suspicion... They even look as if butter wouldn't melt in their mouth... Well, on that point, I can tell you I wasn't taken in!... What bothers me most isn't the grotesque sabre-rattling aspect of this business... although that is disturbing for the more prominent figures in town... as it is for poor Générale Dumesnil herself... And yes, Madame, I would even say that it's disturbing for our unions, our workers, who've come out of this clownish performance looking ridiculous... What's getting at me is your role in all this... what you're really doing in people's homes under the pretence of reading to them... There are even whisperings in the bookshops and libraries, you know... That ad, that basically rather peculiar ad that you ran in the papers...

Arrest me, I say. I look over to the policeman. I'm ready to offer up my wrists. Beloy stops talking, as if gathering himself before pummelling me with more irrefutable accusations. I think he's going to mention Clorinde, who was also compromised by the demonstration. He must be keeping that for the end. The final blow. But no, he doesn't say anything about her. His informers must have been trailing the procession before she joined in. He doesn't know everything. Still, he knows enough to eye me with undisguised contempt, to look me slowly up and down, and tell me that he'll always be implacably, resolutely opposed to troublemakers like me, and he's *got his eye* on me. Which, I see, he certainly has.

After that showdown, I was pretty sure I'd lost any chance of building up a clientele among the town's prominent figures. Yet now, against all expectations, I receive a letter from a very elderly magistrate, a widower who lives alone and can hardly read any more, he says, because his sight's now so bad, and would like to benefit from my assistance. Perhaps from my company too, he adds.

I'm slightly wary. Isn't this going to end up as La Générale and Michel Dautrand rolled into one? Mind you, who can I expect to contact me apart from the elderly, the infirm, the sick and the idle? I've known that from the start. I've known that from the very first. I took the risk. To carry on or to stop. But if I carry on I shouldn't go hoping for new types of requests. Settling into this job means, I fear, settling into repetitiveness. We'll soon see. So I make my way to the home of this president of the court. Pleasant-looking for his age. A double-breasted suit, austerely cut, a tie. A Légion d'Honneur ribbon. A bald head crowned with white hairs. Thick-lensed glasses. Dignity. Courtesy. He starts by telling me he's heard about me, in the most favourable terms, about me and my talent. The quality of my voice. Reading was his life's passion but now, alas, his eyes are failing him. He heaves a sigh. Perhaps I could lend him mine, it would be an incalculable gift, particularly in this, life's twilight, which he's currently experiencing. It would also mean that, once or twice a week, he could escape the cruel loneliness of an ageing magistrate cut off from the things of this world but struggling to let go of them, what with books being the last link that can still connect us to the world when we can't be wholly a part of it ourselves.

I think he put that extremely well. This retired old magistrate must be a cultured man. For the first time I feel it's not up to me to choose what we'll read, the initiative needs to come from him. He must know what he does and doesn't find interesting. What he wants to listen to. Besides, I'm sure he has an extensive library. I glance around the walls of the room, and do indeed see many shelves full of handsomely bound books. Plush décor, a bit dark, a bit cushioned, but orderly, well kept. I keep expecting to see a door open and the inevitable housekeeper appearing. But not a sound, no creak of a door, however slight, no footsteps. Does he live completely alone? He looks in control of his life. In the same way that he looks as if he knows what he wants. I'm sure I wasn't wrong about the choice of books. I let him make suggestions. I tell him I'll make a note of what he wants and do some preparatory work, closely studying the texts he'd like to hear so as to give him the best possible reading of them. I have a special little room at home, all in blue, where I can practise. If I don't have the books, perhaps he could take them from his collection and agree to lend them to me. I'd take the greatest care of them, he can be sure of that.

He looks delighted, overwhelmed. The thought of that blue room has even brought a hint of emotion, a fleeting tenderness to his face. I'm exactly the person he needs. Should we discuss rates? No, he definitely doesn't want to.

Anyway, he lives comfortably on his magistrate's pension and there can be no remuneration adequate to repay the great service I shall be doing him, if, indeed, I consent to accept his choices on the subject of reading matter. Dear Marie-Constance, he says, if you would allow me to do away with pointless formalities and call you by your first name, just as a father would his daughter, dear Marie-Constance, I can tell you're an enlightened woman and, with the experience you must have accumulated, I'm sure you yourself could make excellent choices, but the old man that I am finds the years rapidly overtaking him and some-times thinks there are books, classics, that he's never had time to read, and he wouldn't want to die without knowing them... Oh yes, in terms of reading there are unfulfilled desires, as in other terms... Do you understand? He sighs again, very loudly: Oh, if you'd be so kind!

I tell him I'm at his disposal. Without actually being sure what his point is. It's not long before I understand. He gets up, goes over and takes a beautiful leather-bound book from one of the shelves. Hesitates briefly before showing it to me. Then presents it to me, half opens it, flushing, trembling, palpitating, quivering. It's the Marquis de Sade, he says, it's been here for ever, a family heirloom. It was kept in the attic for a long time, then in the cellar. Now it's here with all the others, because, alas, there's no one but me left in the house to get their hands on it. That's just the point, though. For years I wouldn't allow myself to read it, I didn't dare, my duties required restraint... It's only latterly, with my retirement, time on my hands... but, well, now I can't see... so I thought perhaps...

I'm flabbergasted. But at the same time I feel cornered. Sort of caught in a dilemma in which my professional honour is at stake. If I escape, I fall into his trap. If I refuse, I'm not a *reader*. A reader should *read*, and read out loud, whatever is requested. Please don't let him ask too much! He seems to have opened the book at random. But with de Sade... I take the book carefully. *The 120 Days of Sodom*! There's a bookmark on the page he's showing me and a passage indicated with a cross. This passage, he says, for example, this passage or another... I look at it and, obviously, see some abominations. I try to harden my heart and tell him I'll look into it, I'll have a think about it and we'll see next time. I'm already getting to my feet. He holds me back by my arm. He looks disappointed. Listen, he says very gently but fairly authoritatively, we could have a little trial right now... for me to get an idea... to hear you... to gauge this voice I've been told is such a marvel... Sit yourself down on this sofa here... I'll sit facing you, in the armchair... I'm listening.

So I've been taken in again. I'm surrounded. Flight or professional sangfroid? Marie-Constance, my girl, I think to myself, professional sangfroid it has to be. You've done some acting, you've been through the Conservatoire, you know about the stage and performing, you know about men too, you're not going to let this old toad frighten you. Be brave! I go and sit myself on the sofa. I cross my legs. Adopt an attentive, concentrating expression. Read through my text in silence. I don't believe this! This wasn't random! He chose this deliberately! There are words here which, in all likelihood, will never get through the barrier of my teeth and tongue. Won't get out. What to do? Should I go? The amphibian's eyes are watching eagerly, behind their thick lenses. There's a crushing silence in the room. And, there in that silence, I hear myself read:

A month later, says Miss Duclos, I had dealings with a fucker of an entirely different kind. He was an ageing libertine who, having fucked me and stroked my arse for more than half an hour, drove his tongue into the hole, delving it in there, darting it in there, swirling it and twirling it in there so artfully that I thought I almost felt it in the depths of my entrails. Covering my cunt with one hand, he pleasured himself most voluptuously with the other and, as he discharged himself, drew my anus to him so violently and tickled it so lustfully that I shared in his ecstasy. When he was done, he studied my arse a little longer, staring at the hole he had just widened, and couldn't help himself planting his kisses there once more, then scarpered, assuring me he would come asking for me often, and he was very pleased with me and the way I'd allowed him to spill his come...

I catch my breath. My voice didn't waver or weaken. I didn't stumble. I'm very pleased with myself. He is too, by the looks of things. I'm very pleased with you, he says. I hope you'll be able to come back and carry on.

I wonder anxiously about the possible repercussions. But no, nothing dreadful. He simply makes it clear he'd like us to chat a little longer, to get to know each other better. He tells me about his career, the different posts he held, his wife, who died a few years ago now and whose death left him inconsolable, how difficult it is to dispense justice properly, if indeed, he says, Justice with a capital J means anything, he's not sure it does, after forty-five years exercising it. He seems perfectly civilized and even rather pleasant company. He doesn't offer to show me round the apartment, or to go into detail about his book collection, when I fully expected to have to go deeper into the little corner of 'hell' he must have put together within it. No, here we are, talking away, being utterly *normal*. And after all, if it's normal for him to read and be read texts like the one he's just heard, why should I object? I was absolutely right to accept and harden my heart. A model reader should be a perfectly neutral and biddable instrument. Purely a tool. Purely a voice. Purely transparent. That may well be her limitation, but it may also be her glory. I now feel I'm really getting somewhere with my understanding and implementation of my profession. And at the same time I've achieved undeniable personal progress. When I take leave of my magistrate I thank him and tell him I'll come back. We arrange a date.

The fine weather is back. I've put the crêpe dress on again. Eric will be delighted. He and I have really settled into cruising speed. His mother tells me he's benefiting enormously from these reading sessions, which she refers to as work sessions. If that's true, well, so much the better. In any event, I can see that his mind is increasingly receptive to literature, and particularly poetry, which I was right, I believe, to try to introduce him to in its newest form. Which doesn't appear to have put him off exploring it in older forms. He's inquisitive. He researches. Compares, likens. He's bubbling over with questions, and to think how rarely he opened his mouth in the early days.

When I arrive today, for example, I've hardly sat down before he does just that, asks me a question, and one that immediately strikes me as strange: Madame, could you tell me what *whomsoever* means? I'm all the more astonished because his curiosity is usually far more concerned with the content than the form of literary texts, and he openly claims to have no difficulty with language and vocabulary. So I ask what he means by his question, what allusion, quotation or sentence he's referring to. It's from a well-known poem by Du Bellay:

Or like whomsoever wins the golden fleece...

He's read this famous poem from *Regrets* in one of his schoolbooks and the word brought him up short. I admit to him that I find this strange, because it really isn't very difficult, even for someone unfamiliar with old language, to grasp that *whomsoever* means *whoever*. A demonstrative. I break it down: *whom so ever, who so ever, whoever*. Which is what he would have found had he read the sonnet in a modern transcription. I realize he doesn't know what a sonnet is. I'm not sure I know exactly myself. I gather up my schoolgirl memories. The rules of sonnets, hmm. OK, it must go something like this. Right. I tell him. I explain. He looks very interested. We embark on a discussion about the relative merits of fixed-form poetry and free poetry. Classical poetry and modern poetry. Eric seems to have achieved the feat of getting me learning again in spite of myself (and has done better in this respect than Monsieur Sora) and turning me from a reader into a teacher. His mother's absolutely right to say that these are 'work sessions'. He asks me whether there's such a thing as a modern sonnet. I tell him yes, in Jacques Roubaud's work, for example, and I offer to read him one, from the book I gave him. I look for the page. Here it is:

> *I am a punctilious crab   I am an uneventful mailbag*
> *my field is clear pure swept of every last star I have the*
> *eye's convex globe with velvet all that this instrument*
> *will identify now are its motes of dust*
>
> *I take no risks with silences   I counter only words as*
> *flat as windowpanes rinsed by the rain   and I have*

*a taste for evening   a weakness for dawn there is
never   anything to read in my hand*

He interrupts my reading and, leaning forward in his armchair, takes my hand. There are things to read in your hand,
he says. After the initial shock is over, I reply: Perhaps, as
with any hand. He doesn't let go, inspects it, examines my
palm, my fingers. Why's that called *reading*? I don't know
what to reply, other than: Why indeed? Without relinquish-
ing my hand, he makes a few comments inspired by the
sonnet whose beginning he's just heard. He's not sure he
really understands it, but he was aware of silences, gaps. He
feels, and this strikes me as an extremely astute judgement
on his part, that this poem must have been written to be
seen as much as heard, even more to be seen than heard,
and he points out that his blind friend obviously wouldn't
be able to appreciate it properly. *He*'s lucky he can see. He
takes the book from my knees (his hand brushes over my
dress), studies the page at length. The white bit, the gap,
he says, is meant to be seen. And he adds rather mysteri-
ously: The black is too.

Then he releases my hand, rolls his wheelchair a little as
if wanting to move away, put me at a distance. As you've
worn that dress again, he says, it would be good if you
hitched it up again. I obey. I lift it high up my naked thighs.
We sit in silence. I can barely hear his breathing. Lowering
his head, he then says the following sentence very clearly:
Next time, Madame, if you could come without your
knickers. I wasn't dreaming. He said it.

There's a smell of cool grass rising up from the university campus. I don't want to disturb Roland Sora while exams are on, but I definitely need to ask him what he thinks of my choice of reading material. I find him making some poor female student blanch over a Huysmans text. He slips out with me for a moment and we start walking up and down the corridor while, back in his office, the girl grapples with the text, preparing to say exquisite things about it.

What's good about Huysmans, he says, is he's much more than a naturalist, but he *is* still a naturalist, and in a league of his own. He starts drifting off on to the subject, then asks me whether at the end of the day, after almost a year pursuing my profession, I'm happy with the advice he gave me in the early days. No getting away from it, he says, when all's said and done, the naturalists are the only thing that's true. Only good, solid, dense texts really say anything and, more importantly, they speak the *truth*, they really hook the reader. I think you've seen for yourself, haven't you? I want to please him and agree with his views, but I do have to tell him that I've never found the truth so elusive as it has been since I started this job: it trickles between my fingers, like water I just can't hold in my hands. He shrugs. Water! What does that mean, water? He asks me whether I mean fiction. No, I say, absolutely not, I mean absolutely nothing. He stops his wandering, spins round towards me, gives me that peculiarly bright, twinkling look he has such a knack for when he wants to flush out what he (surely) thinks is my touch of madness.

Maybe he'd like to give me a quick lesson here, on the spur of the moment. But right now that's the last thing I want. I have no desire to feel like that student racking her brains back there in his office. I wish that *he* would understand something I can neither explain nor summarize. Which could possibly be put like this: I like to think I'm choosing passages to read, but they're the ones choosing me. It's a very unusual adventure, a misadventure rather, and I've had all too much proof of that. And that's why his idea that I should hang on to this or that book which would be most appropriate for reading out loud, well, it just doesn't hold together, despite all the respect and affection I owe him. Any book will do, if and when it's spoken by me. And with each of them anything can happen. Which makes me worry that I've chosen the most reckless job in the world. I don't know whether our little town will tolerate me for long.

I've laid out this wonderful argument and it's in the process of falling flat on its face, just like Sganarelle. At least that's what Professor Sora must be thinking; he's still contemplating my face, without trying to hide his commiseration now. I won't have time to tell him about my latest disasters, which I was planning to do. He's going to bring the conversation to an end. He's looking at his watch. His student's waiting for him. He's got these exams on his back. And the summer break beckoning. He tells me that, as I know so much about everything, I'll cope perfectly well on my own. I might even end up opening a school of reading. He has every confidence in my future. Good luck, Marie-Constance!

Not backing away from the risks, then, I return to the magistrate. I've armed myself. I've reread the Marquis, on my own, out loud, in the echo chamber. I braved it all. I even tried out a few pages on Philippe. He liked it very much and announced he'd like to get to know the whole book. He'd always been told the Marquis was boring. That's what people who've never read it say. He turned out not to share this opinion. Philippe has anything but a mediocre mind.

I've come in no-nonsense jeans and a polo shirt, as if for a gym class. Being accustomed to airs and graces, the old man looks rather put out by this. Perhaps to pay me back in kind, he removes his jacket and tie and goes off to put on a silk dressing gown. We're both relaxed. I'm ready to begin. But he doesn't seem to be in any hurry. He looks at the living-room clock, as if keeping an eye on the time, as if waiting for something. We could converse a little first, he says. The word converse makes me melt with pleasure. Very well! I say. What could we converse about? He'd like me to explain how I've trained my voice, how I became involved in acting as a girl, because that's my testimonial. I tell him a bit about it, about the Conservatoire, Godot, Sganarelle. He looks surprised that I played men's roles, asks me why. I say I also often played women: Zéphire, Hyacinthe, Augustine. This seems to arouse his curiosity but also to move him. His eyes cloud slightly behind their lenses. He remembers when he was a child, but of course, he adds, it's starting to disappear into the mists of time. He performed in a play at a prize-giving, and the character he played was called Céladon. He couldn't say what the play was called or the author, in fact it may just have been a middlebrow piece with no known author, but the thing that's still clear in his mind is his costume, or at least one item of his costume, a pink taffeta waistcoat. That pink taffeta waistcoat trills in his head with the sweet, sweet music of memory. Actually, there was a little boy, and he was dressed in gauze, playing opposite him, and his name was Zélamir. He hasn't forgotten the names, they came back to him, as if at the flick of a switch when I mentioned vaguely similar names just now, and he's well aware that those were girls' names: he's not yet completely deaf or completely gaga (those are his words!).

Marvellous conversation, but why this constant eye on the clock? The explanation isn't long in coming. The doorbell rings. The sound of footsteps on the stairs. He goes to open the door. He introduces me to the man who comes in, and he is none other than Professor Dague from the children's neurological unit. There he is, standing squarely before me, full of confidence, a smile on his lips, short hair, smartly dressed. Obviously, he's not in his overalls or in his underpants. But I recognize him perfectly well. The magistrate looks rather embarrassed but is eager to explain this visit: The professor is an old friend, a young friend, rather. We get on very well… we often used to meet at some of the finest dinners in town, when I was still presiding. I thought I could invite him to one of these sessions where you show your talent. I think he'd be utterly charmed... I reply in the briskest of terms: Well, we happen to be old acquaintances too! Precisely! says the professor with the heaviest innuendo, while lighting a cigarette. I'm just wondering how long this performance can go on when the doorbell rings again. Another sound of climbing in the stairwell, noticeably faster. Another opening of the door. Another appearance. Superintendent Beloy this time. I can't believe my eyes. It feels like an ambush. The superintendent gives a slight bow, almost ceremoniously. He's swapped his leather jacket for a lighter one. Perhaps you know each other too? says the magistrate. Indeed we do, replies the superintendent. I remain silent.

A peculiar theatre. And it's not long before the scene is set. What we thought, says the old magistrate, was that the three of us could get together to listen to you. You have such a remarkable organ. Why dissipate the effect it has, its harmonies? Each in our own way, we represent those who are *listened* to in the town. Why shouldn't we come together to start listening ourselves? Why shouldn't we benefit together from your talented readings? It was in this sort of spirit that I've invited my friends here, as I would to a party. The party is you, dear Marie-Constance, your *person*! That's what a reputation does for you!

He pulls aside a large red drape, a sort of curtain that I haven't noticed till now, and the sofa on which I sat last time is revealed at the back of the room, by the bookshelves. I'm sure the arrangement of the furniture has been changed, but perhaps that's a trick of my mind, or my memory. The three of us, he says, are going to sit on this sofa, and you will be in this chair opposite. No sooner said than done. There the three of them are, lined up on the sofa, like dummies, salivating. I feel as if I'm in a firing range at a fairground. And what am I going to do? Read? Read what? I ask the judge. Oh well, he says, the same thing as last time! He's even got the book with the beautiful binding ready, he's taken it off the shelf. He brings it over with a honeyed smile.

It's too much. Professional dedication has its limits. I take my curtsy. Which, with my jeans and polo shirt, is rather ungainly. I make my exit and slam the door.

It seems pretty likely that I'm going to be out of work again now.

Peirene

Contemporary European Literature. Thought provoking, well designed, short.

'Two-hour books to be devoured in a single sitting: literary cinema for those fatigued by film.' TLS

Online Bookshop

Subscriptions

Literary Salons

Reading Guides

Publisher's Blog

www.peirenepress.com

Follow us on twitter and Facebook @PeirenePress
Peirene Press is building a community of passionate readers.
We love to hear your comments and ideas.
Please email the publisher at: meike.ziervogel@peirenepress.com

Subscribe

Peirene Press publishes series of world-class contemporary novellas. An annual subscription consists of three books chosen from across the world connected by a single theme.

The books will be sent out in December (in time for Christmas), May and September. Any title in the series already in print when you order will be posted immediately.

The perfect way for book lovers to collect all the Peirene titles.

> ## 'A class act.' GUARDIAN

> ## 'An invaluable contribution to our cultural life.'
> ANDREW MOTION

£35 1 Year Subscription (3 books, free p&p)

£65 2 Year Subscription (6 books, free p&p)

£90 3 Year Subscription (9 books, free p&p)

Peirene Press, 17 Cheverton Road, London N19 3BB
T 020 7686 1941
E subscriptions@peirenepress.com

www.peirenepress.com/shop
with secure online ordering facility

Peirene's Series

FEMALE VOICE: INNER REALITIES

NO 1
Beside the Sea by Véronique Olmi
Translated from the French by Adriana Hunter
'It should be read.' GUARDIAN

NO 2
Stone in a Landslide by Maria Barbal
Translated from the Catalan by Laura McGloughlin and Paul Mitchell
'Understated power.' FINANCIAL TIMES

NO 3
Portrait of the Mother as a Young Woman
by Friedrich Christian Delius
Translated from the German by Jamie Bulloch
'A small masterpiece.' TLS

....

MALE DILEMMA: QUESTS FOR INTIMACY

NO 4
Next World Novella by Matthias Politycki
Translated from the German by Anthea Bell
'Inventive and deeply affecting.' INDEPENDENT

NO 5
Tomorrow Pamplona by Jan van Mersbergen
Translated from the Dutch by Laura Watkinson
'An impressive work.' DAILY MAIL

NO 6
Maybe This Time by Alois Hotschnig
Translated from the Austrian German by Tess Lewis
'Weird, creepy and ambiguous.' GUARDIAN

SMALL EPIC: UNRAVELLING SECRETS

NO 7
The Brothers by Asko Sahlberg
Translated from the Finnish by Emily Jeremiah and Fleur Jeremiah
'Intensely visual.' INDEPENDENT ON SUNDAY

NO 8
The Murder of Halland by Pia Juul
Translated from the Danish by Martin Aitken
'A brilliantly drawn character.' TLS

NO 9
Sea of Ink by Richard Weihe
Translated from the Swiss German by Jamie Bulloch
'Delicate and moving.' INDEPENDENT

....
TURNING POINT:
REVOLUTIONARY MOMENTS

NO 10
The Mussel Feast by Birgit Vanderbeke
Translated from the German by Jamie Bulloch
'An extraordinary book.' STANDPOINT

NO 11
Mr Darwin's Gardener by Kristina Carlson
Translated from the Finnish by Emily Jeremiah and Fleur Jeremiah
'Something miraculous.' GUARDIAN

NO 12
Chasing the King of Hearts by Hanna Krall
Translated from the Polish by Philip Boehm
'A remarkable find.' SUNDAY TIMES

Peirene Press is proud to support the Maya Centre.

The Maya Centre provides free psychodynamic counselling and group psychotherapy for women on low incomes in London. The counselling is offered in many different languages, including Arabic, Turkish and Portuguese. The centre also undertakes educational work on women's mental health issues.

By buying this book you help the Maya Centre to continue their pioneering services.
Peirene Press will donate 50p from the sale of this book to the Maya Centre.

www.mayacentre.org.uk